BLOODY KNUCKLES

Bloody Knuckles
c. 2014 ThunderDome Press
ISBN: 978-0692023952

Design, and Typesetting by Michael Paul Gonzalez

Printed and Bound by CreateSpace

Cover Photo by Stan Balazia

Interior Photos obtained through Creative Commons License
from SUPERADRIANME on Flickr

Training with the Master, Gym in Black: Black House and the Ethical Manager, and
Bang Muay Thai and the Winged Warrior were previously published at FightWords.com

This book will be released in electronic format, but its primary goal in design is to remind the reader of the simple pleasure of holding the printed work in hand. It's small enough to take with you to spread the word far and wide: the paper book is not dead.
Show it. Share it. Help it survive.

BLOODY KNUCKLES

KNUCKLES

The MMAnthology

Edited by
Michael Paul Gonzalez

THUNDERDOME
PRESS

Table of Contents

Martial Arts Instructor
by Carol Berg

In his gi, with the wide hide-something
inside sleeves, how like an angel
he seems. Appears out of nowhere.
How he holds himself. How he bends.
How he bows to each student and grins.
Mirrors can't hold his image as he flutters
and kicks. Leaps off the ground with bare
feet. Speaks in the language of control.
How committed he is to the sharpened edge.
How he glides. How he looks you in the eye
as he sweeps you off your clumsy feet.

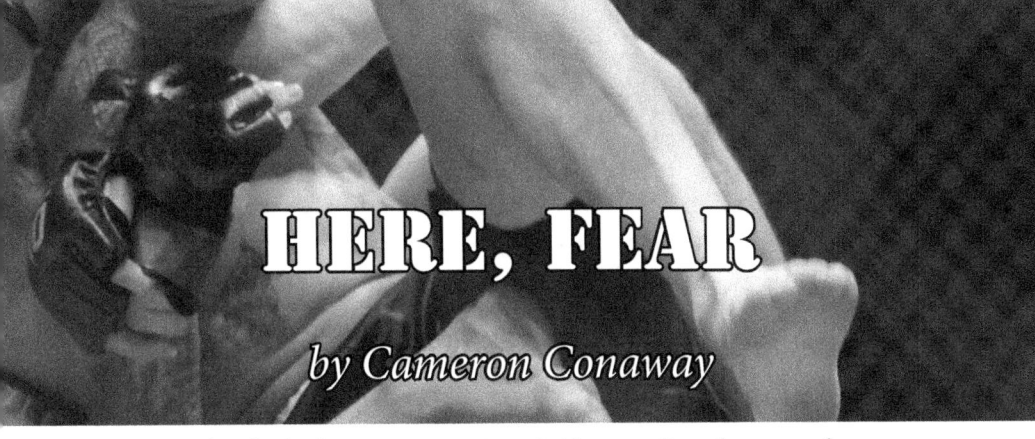

HERE, FEAR

by Cameron Conaway

Did I choke him unconscious? Almost. But that wasn't my intention. My intention was to save myself. I was scared as hell. If I could choke him and leave him lifeless that would mean he couldn't hurt me.

The fight had nothing to do with the end result of the referee raising my hand and everything to do with staying alive. Nothing to do with the choke and everything to do with the subtleties that layered like fibers and led to the choke. To me it had nothing to do with what it looked like and everything to do with what it was: fear. Most of us started fighting out of fear. And many of us continue fighting because through confronting fear we've altered the dynamics of our relationship with it. From that alteration grows something simultaneously empowering and addicting. Whereas fear once made us feel inadequate, it now begets confidence. Our repeated confronting of fear can actually make society view us differently and as something stronger and in this we often embrace a new definition for ourselves. An MMA fighter, they say. A modern-day warrior. A badass. It all comes because we've tamed fear. Once a wild animal gnawing at us, now we treat it like a pet. We feed it. We get annoyed by it. We love it. But what matters most is that we can now walk it rather than be walked by it. We've got the leash.

There has forever been a natural stereotype around fighting and fighters. I say "natural" because it is human nature to try to understand things we don't know based on things we do know. Few people know what it feels like to hear the bolt click, to hear an audience so loud it sounds like silence, to look across an octagonal cage and see a man staring you right in the eyes, a man who has trained for years so that now, in this moment, he can kick your ass.

3

Except that final bit isn't the full truth. The coin's other side is that he's trained for years not so he could break you down but so that he could build himself up. Sure, the residue is that he developed a set of skills that have sport application. But the psychology of an MMA fighter is like a sweep from half-guard – what may look like a tangled mess is so beautifully intricate and multidimensional that it has an inverse. It's that beauty that fighters and true fight fans see. Much of what we love about MMA is in the white space between the leaves; our frustration often comes because outsiders, through no fault of their own, see only the brightly colored leaves.

In this regard, the sport sure hasn't done itself any favors in breaking stereotypes. As MMA has grown so too has the complexity of its imagery, but many new organizations still market themselves primarily with the tried-and-true combination of violence and sex. It works, just look at the ratings for American Horror Story. Hell, it wasn't but sixty seconds after my fights that I found myself holding in one hand a trophy that featured a figurine of a bloody fighter on top and in the other hand free VIP tickets to a strip club. Oh, and I was surrounded by three ring card girls. I didn't want any of that. To be honest, I desperately wanted out of there. I wanted to cry (and later did) and I wanted to get in bed and sleep.

It's easy to see how people could view all this as grotesque, dripping with testosterone and even criminal. The violence they've heard or experienced in real life likely shapes these views. It could conjure up within them stories of robberies gone awry and someone being strangled to death. But who would guess that the fighter on bottom controlling his opponent with a triangle body lock and cinched-in rear naked would likely be the more scared of the two? Who would first see such images for the years of technique contained within them? Who would first see an athletic contest? Likely only the few who have done it. "It's not about winning," my former trainer Renzo Gracie told me:

"...it's about surviving. That's it. All the training we do is simply to survive. If you 'win' it first means you stopped your opponent from attacking you, not because you attacked him. Offense makes the highlight reel but it's actually a form of defense. An incapacitated opponent cannot hurt you."

About those post-fight theatrics whereby the winning fighter totally goes berserk? I've done it. Several times. And that too isn't what it seems.

What seems braggadocios is actually the physical expression of relief. Total unadulterated relief. A celebration of violence or of victory it is not. What it is, for anybody who has achieved any level of success in this sport, is a celebration of everything coming to an end. The grueling training, the fear of losing and of getting seriously injured, the stress a few days prior that made it hard to sleep, in part, because of all the nerve-shits. It's a celebration of being okay, of putting your life on the line and still being alive.

The truer stereotype of fighters is this: most of us came to the sport scared that if a situation arose we wouldn't be able to protect our loved ones or ourselves. Most of us came to the sport broken in some way – broken families, broken relationships, a broken sense of self and self-esteem and confidence. Most of us, through the grind of training and through the trust of our training partners and our coaches, were shaped into far better people than we once were. Society can tout fighters as "badasses" all they want. The truth is that most of us became fighters because we had a wild, pulsating fear trapped inside of us. What's badass is not the crippling heel hook or the flying knee but the work that went into lassoing what once lassoed us.

SUBMITTING THE ABYSS

by Berrien C. Henderson

1: Stand

You already know how this will end.

Each time you get up is a victory unto itself, no matter how much it hurts. It's not about the money because you went years not making any. Keep telling yourself that. Working a J-O-B while on call a few times a week as a sparring partner means you have perks at the gym along with some scratch. When jobs began disappearing at the loading dock, they made it to the last-hired, first-fired folk. Barely in rent, groceries, and gas as it was, and a philosophy major doesn't exactly scream marketable.

Unemployment benefits got you through the better part of a year before drying up and transforming you into a nonperson in the estimation of the Department of Labor.

You come from public assistance and low-rent housing and will be goddamned to go back because spending the better part of childhood in the lobby of the local DHR--PLEASE STAND BEHIND THE BLUE LINE UNTIL YOU ARE CALLED--fostered none too few epiphanies and resentments on your part. They stood in that line and you with them no matter how much pride got squeezed out the corner of your eyes in the middle of the night when they thought you weren't awake, listening.

They:

"OF COURSE IT HURTS! IF IT WERE EASY, EVERYBODY'D BE DOING THIS! YOU AIN'T EVERYBODY!"

At least the van is paid off, and it doesn't cost a thing to park in the gym's lot--out back so it's not a Bondoed eyesore. A handshake and offer to do the gym's towel laundry so you can do your own laundry, and it's all good. "'Til you can get back on your feet," Tony says.

You go through a two-pound tub of whey protein per week along with four dozen eggs. Beans are cheap. So is peanut butter. The microwave at the gym is a Godsend. You have perfected the fine art of a lean, mean poverty diet, and you have never been leaner yourself.

Get back up.

Referee:

"IF YOU DON'T ENGAGE HIM, I'M CALLING THIS FIGHT! THIS IS YOUR WARNING!"

Taste the blood from the broken nose and wince at the ringing in your ear reminding you that you're conscious.

Something crunched in the right side of your face.

This is being conscious. If you are conscious, you can stand.

At least student loan debt can't be repoed.

All kinds of pain, but pain lets you know you're alive.

Stand.

2: Not about the Money

You earn seventy-five bucks per sparring session three times a week. At least you have time to fight five days a week and fill the gaps with fifty-buck days. Take what you can get. Money's tough all around, but so are some opportunities. At least you're well-rounded and can run the gamut of wrestling, boxing, and jiu-jitsu. Worth an extra hundred a week. Maybe.

His name is Brian "Bangarang" Ross. He crushes all kinds of stepping stones and is this close to a professional MMA contract with all the fixings but chose the gym as his training camp since winning the grand prix that got him major notice along with a major purse.

He lives, breathes, and shits fighting and will only ever have enough to get by. This is reality in the circles you all run. Bangarang stands 6'2" weighing 235 pounds of horseflesh but moves like a middleweight. He goes through sparring partners like rag dolls even though fifty percent to seventy-five percent power for him is Godawful.

They needed a solid striker with jiu-jitsu skills, and after a week of partners leaving and fits pitched, this is what you hear:

"Hey, J.P., you want to quit squirreling money and make some quick cash?" says Tony, gym owner and trainer extraordinaire.

You tell yourself it's not about the money, just opportunity, advantageous position.

"Sure."

"Ain't nobody ever knocked down Bangarang training. He thinks he's a regular Pac-Man. Five hundred to anyone knocks him down sparring."

"That's not Pac-Man money," says someone else.

"Yeah, and I ain't paying thirty of my friends to follow me around and play video games between workouts, neither."

Everybody laughs with Bangarang.

"So, J.P., seventy-five bucks just for the session. You know." Bangarang grins at you from the mats in the training cage. "Let me see how those sledgehammers work."

"Sure."

You put on your handwraps, tight on the sore knuckles and hamburger palms from lifting heavy the night before.

"Been making bitches out of guys this week, J.P.," says a guy leaving the mats.

The slightest of tics catches the corner of your mouth.

You don your open-finger gloves.

"Five-minute rounds or three-minute rounds?" says Bangarang.

"Just need one."

"That's what's up."

The cage door closes behind you.

Sledgehammers all the way.

3: Caesura

For the uninitiated, it's a Byzantine series of referrals, of "Yeah, I know so-and-so. How long you train with him?" Time is important along with types of training and cross-training. This lineage of fighters and masters and grandmasters--patriarchy matters. Sons of.

On Tony's suggestion (a guy who knows a guy who…) and after a not insignificant amount of dissembling, you try a few amateur undercards. Sparring partner status keeps the edge honed, but there's something else tickling you, isn't there? It's a lot of trouble to owe favors and owe trainers for ten percent, minimum, on purses. Always a gamble, but you hedge bets every single day just waking up.

Your head bounces off the mat from the elbows and hammerfists, and your brain slips and twists in its own juices while proliferating lightning storms, sprites along the blood-brain barrier.

The abyss closes from the fringes of your vision.

His wrists blur; you can't grab them. He enters your guard, and it's a rookie mistake on your part. You let this happen. Quit thinking, and let. Your. Body. Remember.

Underhook and embrace him and play for--pray for--the advantage.

You had to do something. The van's closing in on you.

So the promoter hands you a spool of tickets once you arrive.

"Okay. You get half of what you sell."

"I thought I'd get a flat rate of 200 dollars for the undercard fight."

"Says who?"

"Omar."

"I fired Omar yesterday. Listen. Shit's gotten a little dicey. I'll be lucky to make a few hundred bucks off this promotion once I figure expenses."

"That's some raw calculus, bub."

"You want to walk, then walk. I don't need no talk-back mouth off of you, J.P. You a college boy, ain't you?"

"Was."

He shoves a spool of tickets at you. "How 'bout you earn some credits in marketing while selling these?"

"What about the other guy?"

He points through the milling patrons.

"He's at his table selling a spool."

"At least you're fair."

"And consistent, too, buttercup. Don't get no paper cuts. Them hands need to be clean."

You sell fifty tickets--two hundred fifty dollars' worth--and discover post-fight your opponent sold forty tickets.

You won by TKO.

In the parking lot afterward, he hurls invectives at his ride. The hood is up and engine not turning over.

"Got jumper cables?"

"Hell no," he says.

You get yours. "Here."

"Thanks, man."

"No problem."

"I ain't working with this amateur hour promoter again."

"Don't blame you."

"Well, you got a tally mark in your record's favor."

"You gave me hell for three rounds. I had to do something."
The two of you share a chuckle, and he shakes your hand.

"Take care."

"You, too."

Why does it feel like a loss?

4: Abiding Place

Tony's previous boarder, Bangarang of all people, left for
greener pastures, and cool-headed guy you are and a steady worker--
great with the laundry, just great--Tony cut you two things: slack and
a deal.

The apartment smells like all the guys who came before-
-several generations' worth of begats in the boxing and MMA
tradition, the stench of frugality and desperation and dedication
redolent with the sweat and mildew and ammonia. A Spartan would
appreciate the place: cot, desk, chair, lamp, hot plate. Stack the
Sterilite containers just so, and you have a pretend chest of drawers.
For two sparring sessions--nearly at half your workload per week--
you can live here.

The one window looks out upon an empty lot.

At least it's not your van.

Opponent:

"GET UP AND DANCE, SON!"

The new venue gives you pause and room to meditate on sea
changes; they always expect you to be the mountain, the session
sparring partner, not to move like the sea and shoot for the clinch
going for matches.

Taking the long view, it was only a question of when.

You kept up with the trail of flyers for amateur bouts with purses big enough to keep you in gas and groceries until three losses in a row (with a spectacularly brutal last fight) found you.

Such matters are cyclic.

Now you understand the losses. The willingness to abide insinuated itself--the myopia of a mental and emotional sticking point over which the shade of Confucius would surely haunt you. Don't mistake equating knocked down to staying down.

You look out the window. Kids chase rats and kill them, hold the vermin by the tails while pearls of blood drip from still-twitching nostrils.

Sometimes violence is its own prize--the acumen for it giving way to status.

All ego and pissing contests anyway.

Perspective is a 235 pound naked ape asserting dominance over you. Something stirs. Toggles. You underhook from guard and back-walk to the fence. It was worth getting pounded a few more times, the sacrifice to regain your feet. Both of you are hot, bloody messes.

Someone:

"*GET UP!*"

You have.

5: Existential

"Why do this to yourself?" says Elle, who runs the gym's pro shop.

You grab leftovers--deli turkey, whole wheat, black beans-- from the fridge before locking it for the night. Her eyes flicker to your jaundiced right jaw.

"It's what I know."

"Why are you even here?"

"That would be the existential question of the day. It's the only job in town suited to my skill set."

"Such as…"

"Philosophy. And working a loading dock until."

"Until?"

"Market forces kicked a few million folks' asses."

Laughing, she grabs a stack of books. "Got to go. Paper to finish and a test to study for."

"Staring into the abyss. Be careful."

"Huh?"

"Nevermind."

You think Elle thinks you didn't work through college at all. Except for the odd work-study program, you sparred same as now. Sixth place in state wrestling conference got you a quarter/partial scholarship, but branching off, cross-training suited, and you found plenty of gyms and dojos.

"There must be more opportunity. People notice things. You come and go, but you don't mess around lifting. And the fighting."

"Sparring."

"That. People say you're good. But--"

"Always somebody better." An arched eyebrow as you rub your jaw. "Opinions and mileage vary."

Elle laughs. "See you later."

"Working tomorrow?"

"Day after tomorrow."

"Bye."

Maybe Elle's right. While eating your leftovers and in the apartment's coverts, you look at the Sterilite container labeled WINTER, and gym sounds wane as silence intrudes. There's a nip in the air again--maybe part of why your jaw's hurting. TMJ is an ironclad bitch.

14

You think deep thoughts about gainful employment at the margins of society--deeper, analytical thoughts about how not to pass guards or give an arm or foot.

What do you have to prove? Miserable in a 9 to 5? More school? Adjunctland? What? Why? How?

You rub your jaw.

Think. Assess. Replay. How not to fuck up in a fight. Minimize by visualizing scenarios.

The security lamps buzz on, layering the abyss with some light.

6: Looking Up

The metal stairs creak. Not uncommon for Tony to come back for something in the office.

A knock at the door, and you get it.

Elle stares back.

"Won't you show me around?"

"Yeah, sure. What brings you up?"

"Left my phone downstairs. Helpless without it."

"Oh, while you spoke, you got the grand tour."

"Maybe you should try stand up."

"Got a middlin' stand up game."

"Funny. So."

"So." She shrugs, then waggles her phone--keys in the same hand, jangling. "Found it."

"Appears so." You step aside.

These quarters were never meant for two, and she bumps the desk, then picks up a dog-eared copy of The Unfettered Mind. "Light reading."

"Passes the time."

"Listen to you. I don't think Zen Buddhist sword philosophy qualifies as light reading," she says.

Surprise forestalls your reply.

"Needed an elective two semesters back. Eastern Philosophy."

"Color me impressed."

"I wasn't the first few weeks."

"Takuan grows on you. Talk about it over dinner?"

"No." She returns the book. "I'd rather talk about something else. After work on Friday?"

"Sure."

"Bye."

"Later."

In the quiet of her absence, you flip through the book. For the moment you two filled the apartment, it was the breath of all Buddhas.

You are glad it swallowed your own voice.

7: Talking Shop

On the back of the flyer tucked partway in your locker, you find this:

Hey. I had a good time the other night. You can put away some food! Really good time. --Elle

Announcing the Tri-County "Blood in the Cage" Grand Prix!
1st Place Purse of $5000!
2nd Place Purse of $1000!
Guaranteed!

You call the contact number, and when you approach Tony, you find the back of the line.

"I got another fight that day," Tony says.

"Walked out alone before."

"Well, I hate it, J.P. I do. I'd rather not commit than over-commit if you get me. Felipe's got a huge fight."

"Just grateful you've given me a place at the table. Plus, Felipe's put in plenty of time."

Tony says, "I'll see about setting it up. Got your labs?"

"Yeah." You show the edge of an envelope.

"The gym will pay your entry fee. All I ask is ten percent on whatever you win, but I'll waive the twenty percent for promotion given prior engagements. Right, Felipe?"

"Right, boss!"

"That's generous, but--"

"Listen, you got four weeks until this grand prix."

"Yes, sir."

"And quit with the 'yes, sir' shit."

"All right."

"Here's deal: You work five days a week next two weeks. Whatever extra training you yourself squeeze in, do. Two weeks before the tournament, we'll boot camp. What about your weight?"

"210."

"Steady?"

"Rock."

"Good. Bet you shopped for husky jeans as a kid."

"Just look at me now."

"Ha! So, the offer?"

"Point me in the right direction and take off the collar."

He claps you on the shoulder. "That's the spirit!"

Grind.

Slogfest.

A month of hell, but you smile.

8: Weak Legs

Speed bags wuurrmm. Heavy bags creak on their chains and shiver from cold, heartless poundings. Guys hit the mats. Each other. You finish stretching, then help Felipe with sparring practice. In the gym proper, beyond the plate glass windows of the fighting studio, customers come and go. Elle sets a meal replacement bar on your leftovers in the fridge, but you pretend not to notice.

Tony motions you in close. "J.P., listen, I might've been born at night, but not last night."

"Care to clarify?"

"No disrespect, but you and Elle."

You shrug.

"I got no problem in general with it."

"But you got one in particular."

"J.P., you're training, and hard. We've talked about Felipe's fight, but I still need you committed. And fast. Mean. This tri-county tournament's no joke and a great opportunity. Watch for weak legs."

"I'll take it under advisement."

"Snake mean, son."

Elle throws a glance from the counter.

"Gotcha."

Later that night, Elle's forgotten her cell phone again. The abyss hovers two weeks away tomorrow; you avoid it across town for dinner but find it back at her apartment. She counts your bruises and scars from places you shouldn't have been.

"Serious about the tournament?" Elle says.

"Yes."

She catches herself, switches direction. "It's just…"

"You gave me the flyer."

"I gave you a courteous note on a flyer that was stuck under my windshield wiper." She sidles closer. "I didn't mean it that way."

"Let's talk about this later."

"Maybe."

"I don't like guesswork."

"Neither do I."

She takes down her ponytail, and raven mane engulfs your head and face--a different kind of abyss, and you welcome it as she mounts.

9: Grand Prix

It goes fast.

Three five-minute rounds, a minute break between. Eight fighters helm the light heavyweight division.

Your strategy is simple: Finish fast and decisively. Longer fights mean more sustained damage; both sides lose in a protracted battle.

Two wins land you in the semi-finals.

The referee didn't get to one of Bangarang's opponents fast enough. The poor guy was still seizing when they carted him out of the cage on a backboard.

This is not sparring practice.

There is no fifty percent--no seventy-five percent.

Blood in the cage, indeed.

Keep moving. Catch your breath. He has to work hard to pummel you so much.

Finals. Only winning matters now. Judges keep score for a reason. All warfare is based on deception, so trust your boy Sun Tzu.

The semi-final fight went two rounds plus four minutes, thirty-eight seconds of the third round. So much for quick finishes.

The purse you are guaranteed... well, it was never about the money.

The leader board changes--your name beside Bangarang's.

She:

"I DIDN'T SHOW UP TO WATCH YOU FAIL!"

You are tired and hurt.

So is Bangarang, still heavier and stronger.

He knows what you're packing. Exploit. Capitalize. Own.

Sharpen your mind on the whetstone of strategy, and...

He breaks his hand on the crown of your head only because you had the presence of mind to offer it instead of fading and taking it on your right orbital, already a mess. As soon as he switched stances and tucked that hand closer to his chest, you knew. Feints, a shoot, and a slam. The world goes cold and quiet--tunnel vision with the abyss closing in from the periphery. Elbows. Hammerfists.

You rain hell upon him.

Bell.

Only the end of the first round.

Round two presents no takedowns for either fighter. If he wants to go bang...

Jabs and crosses and hooks and leg kicks.

Strike the four corners--weaken and wither and wear down.

Christ Almighty, but Bangarang has found another gear. Both of you slip in blood, and the crowd cheers its money's worth.

That's all right, even walking on buckling legs to your respective corners. A minute to rest. Final round. Cakewalk.

You can't physically smile glimpsing Elle in the crowd, can you? Not when the right side of your face feels bloated and bursty and faraway.

Elle turns her head.

You don't blame her.

10: Cornered

Why are you here?

You stare at *it*.

Every technique forwards the fight's narrative; the denouement means winning. Oh, losing is an option. Highlight reels are full of losers.

Bushido?

You don't have heart, you don't have shit. Bullshit-o, that's what you got.

How fucking much do you want to breathe? Pussies will never be heroes.

It stares back.

Endorphins wear off. Adrenaline dumps. Opponents can be bled, broken, submitted. Never look into the eyes--just the chest, heart, soul. Close your eyes when you clinch and takedown. It's all in your head, and the old German was on to something, so you take him at his word.

There are few problems that can't be solved through the proper application of a rear-naked chokehold.

You have stared into the abyss with two other opponents today.

You cannot unbreak a nose or harvest cauliflower ears.

Only collect tally marks like the test etchings on the tang of a *katana*.

Because it will always stare back.

11: Last Round

There's no hate in Bangarang's eyes. He even blows you a kiss. You wink back.

The ref brings you in.

"FIGHTERS, ARE YOU READY?!?"

Five more minutes.

That's all.

You already know how this ends.

Und wenn du lange in einen Abgrund blickst, blickt der Abgrund auch in dich hinein.

--Friedrich Nietzsche

TRAINING WITH THE MASTER

by Michael Strayer

Focus.

The sound of leather hitting leather bounced across the room. Grunts, and the hiss of breath, and the squeak of bare feet on mats—all combined to form a ceaseless cacophony of visceral noise, a rat-a-tat-tat crescendo, repeating itself over and over, again and again…

Focus.

The students faced off in pairs, dressed in shin-guards and thick leather gloves, some with mouth guards, some moving fast, some slow, punching and kicking and then defending, each sweaty and intent…

Cross—hook—low kick! Defend… Uppercut—hook—high kick! Repeat…

"Focus!"

Bas Rutten's Dutch-inflected voice rang out above the din of training. "You have to focus…" he said. "All right that's enough." The students rested. They watched their teacher—thick-set, bald, his brow heavy, his neck muscled. At 48 years of age, Bas Rutten strikes an imposing figure. Power seems to radiate from the former fighter. It pulsed through the room like a wave of electricity when he demonstrated the proper way to punch, or as he seized a student round the neck and fired a quick knee to the side, stopping just shy of contact.

But even shadowboxing, the force of his attacks could be felt. There's a precision to his movements that only comes from uncountable hours of repetition, coupled with decades of experience competing at the highest level. As a three-time King of Pancrase and the former UFC Heavyweight Champion, Bas Rutten has experience in spades. He is a master fighter, retired on a 22-fight win streak, and watching him perform he could never be mistaken as anything less.

"Focus," he was saying. "I know it's hard. But if you can't do it in here, how will you do it in a real fight? You need good accuracy to throw an effective punch." He pointed to his lower abdomen. "You can punch me here all day, it won't do a thing. I'm not kidding. But here—" he raised his finger to his solar plexus "—here, and boom, it's done."

His Netherland roots shine through in every word. He pronounced 'hook' as 'whook' as he relayed instructions for the next series of drills. The class continued. The sound of training—of breath gasping through teeth, of gloves absorbing gloves, of shin-guards striking thighs—picked up speed. And over it all, piercing the clamor, Bas's voice:

"Block, block, Punch! Punch, punch, kick! It should be that fast. Don't forget to keep your hands up."

Combinations followed by counterattacks, back and forth. To an outsider, it might have looked like dancing, one student moving forward, the other back, and then—suddenly—the roles were reversed, the defender advancing behind a one-two combination finished with a lower inside leg kick. And then the dance began anew.

"Focus," Bas intoned. "Focus is the key to power. Plant your feet, cock your fist and, Bam!" He twisted his body, launched a right cross, his fist slicing through the air. As he did, the Chinese character for Chi—or Life Force, from which all power is derived—tattooed on his palm could be seen. "Make sure the weight of your body is behind it," he said. "Because if it isn't, then what's the point?"

Between drills Bas walked amongst his students, correcting posture, observing, pointing out mistakes. Rest periods were frequent, but short-lived. He told anecdotes of his fighting life, cautionary tales of sparring with Dan Henderson, stories of cunning regarding his defeat of Tsuyoshi Kohsaka. He talked of his karate roots, streetfighting as a bouncer, the importance of a straight wrist.

"Your fist is like a tooth pick I always say. If you're trying to break it in your fingers by pushing down and it's completely straight, you can't. But bend it just a little, and it snaps."

24

The class went on, the drills increasing in complexity and pace. At the hour's end, Bas told everyone to stop and gave a brief lecture on the value of practice. Again, he mentioned focus.

"When I was in the Thai Boxing gym for the first time," he said, "I dropped my hands and the guy knocked me down. I told myself: 'That will never happen again.' So what did I do? I went home and for four hours I stared at the mirror and held my hands up—throwing punches." He calls them panches. "My wife thought I was crazy… I told her, 'You'll see.' Four hours, I practiced that night. That takes focus. Drive. The next day I went to the gym and cleaned the place out."

He gazed at his class and smiled. "And guess what? If I can do that, so can you."

Elite MMA, where Bas trains and holds his classes, is situated on the basement level of a health and fitness center in Thousand Oaks, California. There's a cage with matted floors to the immediate right of the entrance, a gym section straight ahead—a large tire, double-end bag, various exercise machines, a barbell, dumbbells, medicine balls—and hallways extending in two directions: one to a large matted room where jujitsu and mixed martial arts classes are led, the other to the lockers. Across from the lockers is Bas's office: a tiny, unassuming room with a desk, computer, microwave, coffeemaker, television, tapes.

I drove out there on a Tuesday evening in May, to take a class with Bas and interview him afterwards.

Bas sat at his desk, still sweating, blew his nose, and rubbed his eyes. He yawned. Normally a vivacious and stimulating presence wherever he went, Bas had contracted an infection recently and the antibiotics were making him tired.

"I tell you," he said. "I never felt like this before… It's like gravity man, pulling me down."

Behind him on the wall was the promotional poster of his fight with Kevin Randleman for the UFC Heavyweight belt. That was on May 7th, 1999, and today the charismatic warrior known as "El Guapo" still looks much the same—bald, smirking, and strong.

"What first drew you to fighting?" I asked.

"Drew me?" he said.

"Yes. Fighting's a calling. When did you first feel the tug?"

"As a kid," he said. "I had eczema you know, very bad, very bad skin... And so I was the one they picked on. So there was that. And then in... 1976. Me and my brother snuck into a movie, Enter the Dragon with Bruce Lee... And I remember seeing him [Lee] up on that screen and thinking, Man if I could just be like that, nobody could mess with me.

"I started doing Taekwondo and one of the neighbor's boyfriends—he practiced and was into that, so he took care of me. And then when I was 20—21 I got into karate... And it was really good, because I was still a kid... I was crazy. Out of control. So when I started karate that was a good thing for me to focus... I loved absorbing techniques. Katas, that was my thing. But when I would run them, man I would run them... Exploding with every punch and kick...

"But I really understood that kata won't me make a good fighter. And we'd have sparring classes, and I was dropping everyone there and I thought, Ooh, that's not good. I need to go somewhere I can get competition. I went to Thai boxing. And Thai boxing really taught me to fight. I got dropped the first class right away with the liver shot, I was messed up, you know... But like I said, those four hours in front of the mirror changed me. And I've always been like that... If I can't do it, I can do it tomorrow. I'm very driven with everything I do.... Martial arts gave me that focus."

From kickboxing, Bas progressed to MMA, fighting in some of the sport's earliest incarnations. In Japan he won the coveted King of Pancrase event three times, competing against MMA pioneers like Frank and Ken Shamrock, Guy Mezger, Vernon White, and Masakatsu Funaki. When he entered the Ultimate Fighting Championship in 1999, he was already hailed as one of the greatest fighters on the planet. Since then, he's garnered international acclaim for his violent, technical striking, his use of the liver shot, his easygoing, excitable persona, and is widely credited with having

26

transformed the definition of a heavyweight fighter.

He fidgeted as he spoke, his hands shifting between the items on his desk—keys, phone, files, phone, keys. Behind him, his image in the poster seemed to wink.

"The thing with fighting," he said. "It's all about the set-up. I always say this: a right straight to the head is a very simple punch. But it's also very easy to defend. The trick is to set it up in such a way he doesn't see it coming... That's the trick in fighting. Then you knock him out. It's the same thing with rolling... Everybody can do a Figure-Four (key lock), I always say. The trick is to go there undetected. You have to be creative.

"But they can take anything, people... Never forget about adrenaline. That's why the set-up is so important."

He leaned back in his chair.

"Adrenaline," he said. "I never believe somebody can fight unless they've actually been in the ring. And I mean a real fight. Sure you have guys who look good in the dojo. I guarantee in the gym there's a guy who beats up Jon Jones... But in the arena... in the fight... Fighting in the dojo or in training, it's completely different than the real thing... It's like..."

"It's transcendent..." I said. "Soulful..."

"Exactly," he said. "If you can bring the gym to the fight, that's the magic. You have to control your nerves. But I tell them, I tell my fighters: forget about nerves. Because once that bell rings..." He made a gesture of closing with his hands. "It all just goes away... I always thought I did better in the actual fight."

For a moment his eyes grew wistful, and a contented smirk stretched across his face. He spoke of his first fight—a $2,000 prize— and of his bout with Kevin Randleman and the sound of tens of thousands of screaming fans. He reflected on the old days of the sport, the original UFC tournaments, those three fight, bareknuckle contests sans rule and regulation.

"People ask me if I'd like to fight in the first UFC and I'm like 'No!' No referee? Nobody to stop the fight? So if he knocks me out and I'm out and there's nobody to stop it and he decides to throw five extra punches I'm gonna walk away with a speech impediment..?

I said… 'I got a daughter, I'll do it if there's a referee.'"

He became silent at the mention of his daughter. He'd been away on fight business for her birth and when he speaks of her he remembers those lost times, missed Christmases, holidays spent ringside while the family watched at home.

He perked up. "I'm not one of those guys who says that when I fight I prepare for war, I'm prepared to die. If there's any possibility of death, I tap or I stop." He laughed. "I got a family, you know? I wanna live to be a hundred years old.

"The thing is," he said, serious once more, "I'll never be in that situation, because nobody trains harder than me. My thing was that if I fight you, I promise you I have more stamina. Nobody did the crazy things I did. And I really worked hard at it… I always tried to not be a slugger… I liked to be clean…"

"What do you think about the rule changes?" I asked.

"Rule changes?"

There had been several rule changes since Bas's time in the sport. I was thinking particularly of the rule stating that you cannot knee or kick to the head of a grounded opponent (grounded meaning that any part of the body other than the soles of the feet is touching the canvas).

"I would love to see them re-evaluate that," he said, clapping his hands. "That bullshit rule with the hands on the ground? Fighters take advantage of that. That's so weak. I hate it. I would even say take out elbows and keep the knees to the face (on the ground). It's only lately that you see guys knocking guys out with it (the elbow). And I'm not saying that's bad. That's cool stuff. But it's one knock out in 500 fights with an elbow. I think I can count on two hands fights that ended with the elbow knock out. Most of the time it's cuts. Which is crazy. On the street, would you stop at a cut? No… It's not a good win. It's not clean."

"Where do you see the sport going in the future?" I asked.

"Well what you're seeing is not a lot of submission victories anymore… Most of the time it's ground and pound now, with maybe attached to it a submission—rear naked choke, that kind of thing. That you still see. But otherwise I think for fighters, a lot of them want a decisive win. They wanna knock them out. And I think that's what's behind today's fighters… they want to keep it on the feet, knock the guy out, because now I won. On the ground, sorry, but there's a lot of stale guys who won't take risks on the ground… They just lay there, control, little punch here, little punch there. That's not what people wanna see. That's not how fighters wanna win. They want clean victories."

Bas Rutten has a positive outlook on today's fighters. Perhaps his statements are mostly true; or, perhaps, they're a projection of his own ideologies… His personal record, after-all, only included three decision wins, with 14 submissions and 12 knockouts.

He went on.

"I still see the sport getting bigger. Because people are always gonna wanna see the biggest bad-ass on the planet." He spread his hands. "Which, let's face it, is the mixed martial artist—not the boxers or the Thai boxers. It's the guy who knows it all."

He smiled. He yawned and rose from the desk. He faced an empty gym. The smell of eucalyptus from the sauna permeated the building and beneath that the smell of rubber and sweat.

We walked together through the gym, out the door, and into the warm California night. The sky over Thousand Oaks was a velvet lilac color. He stood in the parking lot and gazed at the darkening horizon. He took a deep breath, filled his lungs, exhaled.

A force surrounds him, this aging warrior. He has sacrificed, fought. He has bled and drawn blood. He walked—swift, purposeful steps. The sun set. He got in his car and drove off.

There is magic. Bas Rutten knows this.

DOWN BENEATH PARADISE CITY

by Nik Korpon

Jeremy sets his gym bag beside the row of empty kegs and plops on a bucket of drained grease. The air in this basement tastes of moldy sawdust and fermented beer. In the larger room next door is the muted smack of knuckles tenderizing face, heard between lulls of drunken shouting. The crowd's pretty small tonight, and the rockabilly playing the Paradise City bar upstairs won't have to turn up the amps too much to mask the sound of men beating one another into bloody knots. He pulls out a roll of athletic tape and flexes his fingers, then starts wrapping a sponge in his grip. Gus said the man he's fighting is an architect or foreman or something. He also said he's a prick, but an honest prick, so Jeremy leaves the roll of coins in his bags tonight. He hopes the man knows it's lights out in the fourth, so he won't have to take out the coins or the baton.

The door swings open, pushed by a thick man with DIRT ROAD tattooed across ragged knuckles.

'Evening, beautiful,' Rollo says.

Jeremy nods and pulls the tape tight around his wrist, tearing the end with his teeth. He holds a fist up to Rollo, who smacks it five times with his palm.

'Cynthia out of town?'

'I said don't talk about her.'

'Your hands are soft, so I figured you'd been using Curel to jerk off again. Not trying to say nothing about your lady.'

'Then stop talking about her.' She'd had her wild days like anyone, but hers veered whole hog into shameful. The crack didn't help, either. Jeremy points at his ear, indicating the chunk missing from Rollo's. 'If you're shaving your ears, might want to hit up your neck, too. I can't tell where your pubes stop and face starts.'

31

'Does the joke circuit get real quiet when you're fighting?'

Jeremy starts taping his other wrist as Rollo hangs his bag on the handle of the keg refrigerator. Jeremy bites back a laugh. 'Sorry, I've got some shit going on. Can I bend your ear a minute?'

When the crowd outside explodes with shouts and yelling at the sight of blood, Jeremy imagines it's really for him and can't hold that laugh any longer.

'Are you funny on purpose or does it just happen naturally?' Rollo snatches the tape from Jeremy.

'I'm not done with that.' He grabs for it but the big man's hand slaps Jeremy's ear before he can react.

'Told you you're dropping your left.'

The door pops open again. A squat man with the ridged forehead of a pug who used his face as a speed bag ducks inside for a second and tugs on Jeremy's arm. 'He's wobbling a fierce one. Get to your getting.'

'Relax, Gus. I'm coming.' Jeremy just holds his palm out. Rollo drops the tape in it.

'So, how did you go all van Gogh?' Jeremy wraps the tape quickly, the layers doubling up instead of edging past the underlying one like they should. The padding is lumpy across his knuckles but he doesn't have time to care.

Rollo strips off his shirt. In the dim lighting, the sharpened chicken bone scars on his chest are almost purple, but the pyramid and all-seeing eye tattooed from armpit to armpit is impossible to conceal, or cut away. His knuckles fared better, but they also weren't done with a modified Walkman by a lieutenant in the Black Guerilla Family. 'You know the story. Beigler says the money's due Tuesday morning, I get there Tuesday night, Otis takes exception on his behalf.'

Jeremy folds his shirt over the edge of an empty box. 'Otis took part of your ear because you were a couple hours late paying?'

'In my defense, I'd just worked a double and fell asleep.'

'Hell of a late fee.' Jeremy takes a few tentative swings at his shadow-head, swinging his arms in circles and feeling his shoulders slowly loosen. He relaxes his eyes, staring into the blank space behind the paint sloughing off the cinder block wall, rearranging the nothing into the man's ribs, watching them open as he rears back with a hook, watching his left hand drop before he throws a right cross. Imagining everyone who's been with or talked about Cynthia, Jeremy uncorks a flurry of hooks to the man's ribs, denting his body like a soda can lying in the gutter. He hears his name and blinks a few times.

'They're calling for you.'

Jeremy takes a deep breath, spins on his heels and heads out.

'Hey,' Rollo calls. Jeremy pauses. 'If you need anything I'm ear for you.'

Jeremy gives a thin smile then nods and leaves. As he weaves through the bodies swollen with 50-cent Natty Bohs, all he can think is he hopes to fuck that his man knows which round is the fourth.

Red Fabian, the man pegged as referee for the night, stands above a lump of meat sprawled over the floor, holding up Dwaine's arm as the victor. Long slashes of blood striate the concrete around them. Jeremy squints and he's pretty sure that shiny little dot is a canine tooth. Two lugs in flannel hunker down and sling the prone man's arms over their shoulders, dragging him out of the room. Dwaine gives Jeremy a gapped and bloody smile, though Jeremy's surprised the man can even see out that eye.

'Rollo'll bleed your eye for you.'

Dwaine claps him on the shoulder.

'There's a razor in my bag if you don't have one.'

'I'll wash it off.'

'Just keep it.'

Jeremy steps in the square of concrete masquerading as a ring. Four spray-painted streaks show the crowd—who doubles as ropes—how close they can get, and the posts keeping the ceiling aloft standing in for corners. Though it's a step up from sparring with his road crew buddies on lunch break and a far cry from breaking faces in the alley, it isn't quite what Jeremy envisioned when he walked into Curtis's Gym fifteen years ago. The envelopes from Mr. Beigler help supplement road work and Cynthia's secretary paycheck, but still.

Red leans up against a post with a cigarette drooping in his mouth. He nudges a friend in the ribs and laughs, then takes a long belt from a plastic bottle. With something that could approximate boredom, he eyes the fighters warming their muscles as Gus scatters sawdust to soak up the blood.

Jeremy eyes up the other fighter. He's tall enough to feel the need to duck when walking beneath low ceilings, but thick ropes of muscle twist and stretch when he swings his arms, making his lanky frame appear more feral than comic. Man doesn't even look like has callouses, much less a gnarled forehead from time in the ring. He strings together a jab-cross-hook combo, not even throwing a glance toward Jeremy.

'You said he's an architect?' he says to Gus.

'Think so.'

'He looks like a cocksucker.'

'Definitely so.'

Red strolls into the center of the ring, yelling to the crowd to shut up their dick-traps if they want to see any action.

'Y'all know the rules,' he says, more to the drunks than the fighters, 'so you got two minutes til the books close.'

The other fighter swings his arms in circles and throws his head back and forth, then comes close to Jeremy. 'I know you?'

Jeremy shrugs, squats a few times. 'Sure.'

'All right,' Red says to them. 'If you got something on the side, at least give these people something to talk about first. Otherwise, good luck.' He checks the inside of their fists for anything hidden then backs away as the fighters raise their hands, waiting for the say-so.

'You live on Conkling?'

Jeremy drops his guard.

'Yeah, I'm Bill Stoker.' He extends a taped hand and smirks. 'I used to know Cynthia back in the day.'

Jeremy lashes out with a right and catches Bill just beneath his eye. The crowd explodes with shouts.

Jeremy closes the space between them, throwing a cross then hook aimed for Bill's ear. Bill slips it and sidesteps, moving to the left while sending out a few exploratory jabs. The last one skips off Jeremy's forearm, and when he sees Bill lean forward off-balance, he sets his feet and pivots from the hip, aiming at a point three inches behind Bill's forehead. The impact of knuckle on skull shivers up his forearm. Bill stumbles back and Jeremy advances, throwing two more rights before Bill finds the concrete.

'Say one more thing about her and I'll hit you til you see black.'

Bill blinks a few times and tries to spit out the blood but it just dribbles down his cheek. He waits for Jeremy to step back before standing up and uncorking a jab-cross-cross that vibrates in Jeremy's stomach. The ring shrinks a few feet as the drunks shove forward. Jeremy flicks his head to the side, clears the dots floating in the before him and attacks. Jab, cross, jab, jab, hook. Bill's eyelid busts open, adorning his face with blood curtains. Jeremy's lip splits and each cross sends a new arc of blood at Bill. Cross, cross, uppercut, uppercut. Cheeks swell and ear ring. Blood mixes with sweat and covers their bodies in war-paint.

After an eon of pain, Red shoves his way between the two, catching knuckles on his temple.

'Motherfuckers I called time twenty seconds ago!'

He pushes them back to their corners. Gus tries to massage Jeremy's shoulders with slaps.

'The fuck you doing, kid? You're going to punch yourself out, you don't pace yourself.'

Jeremy spits a glob on the floor. 'Just give me some water.'

'Never make it to the fourth, is all I'm saying.' Sal hands him a plastic cup and stained towel. Here, there's no adrenaline 1:1000, Avitene or Vaseline. Just sawdust and water.

'Christ, Gus. Everyone know about this?'

'Only them who need.'

Red calls for them and Gus points at the ring.

Jeremy makes his way in measured steps, taking labored breaths through nostrils that are quickly closing. He hasn't seen his face but if Bill's is anything to judge by, he's pretty as an unwiped, prolapsed asshole. He raises his hands.

Red says go.

The two circle each other, trading more head dekes than solid hits for a good minute. The crowd throws their cups and cans in place of the punches. He edges close enough to let Bill get in a few good shots, but slips them with a glance or forearm. After another minute of hanging back and pulling half-shots, Bill manages to get in close and land a thick hook to the ribs. He grapples tight with Jeremy.

'What the hell are you doing?'

'Don't fuck with me until the fourth.' Jeremy lodges knuckles just below Bill's solar plexus. The wheeze is audible.

'What's the fourth?' Bill pushes back and takes an off-balance pot-shot.

'They said you were okay.' He plants his lead and drops a cross on Bill's cheek.

Bill stumbles back, stunned for a second. He raises his hands but skips around Jeremy slowly, his head cocked like he's deep in thought. Another twenty seconds. 'You shitting me?'

Jeremy slaps a hand against him. The crowd showers them with boos.

'You son of a bitch.' Bill drops his hands all together. 'You're lying down just like Cyn used to.'

Jeremy stops stock-still, then charges with an overhand haymaker. Bill's hands aren't fast enough and he catches it right on the jaw, spinning him around into another wild overhand. He falls to a knee and Jeremy cocks back like he's splitting wood but Red wraps his arms around Jeremy's waist and whirls him aside.

'Can't you shitbirds hear?' He pushes Jeremy at Gus and shoves a cigarette between his lips.

Gus is nothing if not pissed. He doesn't even offer water or the towel. 'Calm your ass down.'

Jeremy starts to spin toward Bill but when he sees Otis standing beside the steps to upstairs, he catches himself.

Gus lays his hands on Jeremy's shoulders, looks up at him. 'We both know the score, and we both need the money.'

Breath courses from Jeremy's nose. He can't stare at anything but Gus's cauliflowered ear. He can see Cyn with her glass pipe at a party, folding the blanket over their couch, sucking her way out of a possession charge, making omelets in her terry-cloth robe.

'Yeah.' He takes a deep breath through his mouth. 'Yeah, we're cool.'

Gus slaps his cheek. 'You're a good kid, Jerry. So be one.'

Jeremy just looks over his shoulder at Otis, who whispers into Chet's ear then nods toward the back keg room. Beigler, probably.

Red's voice rings out behind him. 'Come on, now.'

Just one more round.

He lets his arms hang loose at his side while approaching Bill. We're all friends here.

Bill smiles and shows the blood on his teeth. 'I'm going fuck you like—'

Bill's tooth is cutting through his skin before he realizes he swung. Two, three, four in the mouth. Bill's tooth sticks in his wraps. His cheek splits in two spots, his lips halving in a great gush. Bill doesn't fall until Jeremy's arm begins to hurt, but only goes to a knee. Jeremy takes two steps and unleashes a hook straight into Bill's ear. The sounds spreads through Jeremy like a rock in a still pond. Again. Again. Again.

His arm is back but Gus and Red are on him and he's tumbling to the ground. He blinks and sees the rafters of a shitty bar in Highlandtown. He tastes blood, feels a vicious throbbing in his wrist. He looks to the side and sees the side of Bill's head shining red. His arms are punched numb.

Fourth round you put him down. Not until the fourth round.

This is the third round.

Jeremy scrambles to his feet and shoves his way toward the door. He can grab Cyn and they can go stay with her mother on the shore or go to Richmond. They can cover the windows with foil for the next three years.

Otis grabs his arm. He feels the nerves screaming. 'Stairs are broken, boy.'

'Tell him I'll make it up.' Jeremy's panting and hates himself for it.

Otis spins him around and pushes him through the edge of the crowd with a heavy hand. 'He don't care much for "Don't shoot the messenger."' The keg-room door swings open, Chet standing aside like a macabre maitre'd.

A man leans against the refrigerator door, cleaning his fingernails with a straight razor. The sweatsuit does nothing to hide his $100 haircut. He points a thick finger at the chicken grease bucket. 'Sit.'

'Mister Beigler, look, I can explain—'

'It's my turn to talk, son.' He ambles toward Jeremy. 'We need to have us a word.'

This story has been expanded into the novel
Fight Card: Punching Paradise
available through www.fightcardbooks.com

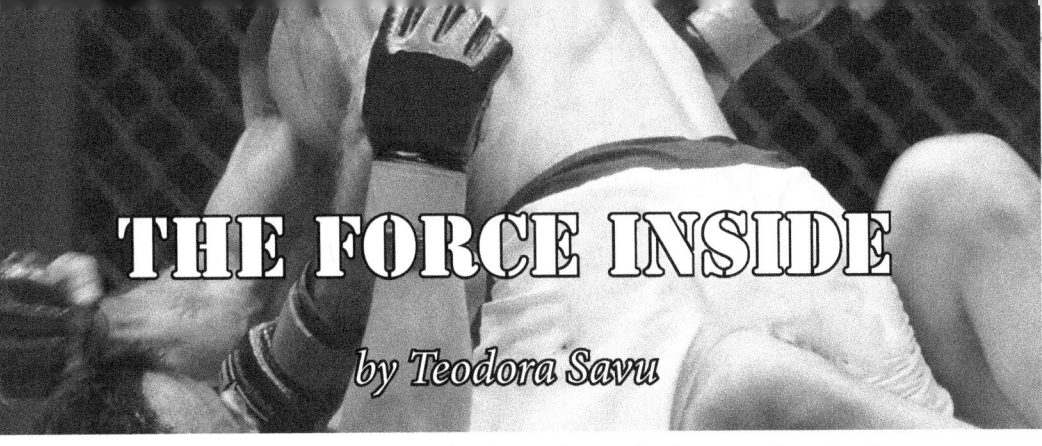

THE FORCE INSIDE

by Teodora Savu

We spend a lot of time thinking about the future, planning it, trying to predict it. 'Future' is an ambiguous notion, but all of us have to admit that it is the home of our strongest fears and our deepest hopes. 'I want to be a football player,' the boy next door may say. 'I want to be a figure skater,' you may hear a little girl giggling towards her mother. Most of our future resolutions imply ourselves, our abilities and our passions. These kids who want to become famous athletes, you can probably see them running on the field or skating on the ice rink all day long, falling, rising again and going on. They would meet many people who'd laugh in their faces and tell them that they are not good for these sports. But what they would have to do in that moment would be to smile politely, but secretly ignore those mean words.

I had been told before that martial arts were not for me, that I was too nice and that I couldn't hit somebody, so I had to pick a brighter sport, like tennis or badminton. Even I knew that TaeKwonDo was not the perfect sport for me, but this didn't mean that I couldn't do it. I had seen a friend of mine doing it and I wanted to try it as well. I truly wanted to do it.

Everybody has their limits, those fine lines that define them. They advance towards them and when they finally touch them with their foot, they stop and say 'that's it'. That's it... because that seems to be their highest level; it looks as if behind those lines, there is nothing but a wall. Very few people realize that this concept is totally untrue. There may be a wall, but with enough force, even a wall can be knocked down. And the ones who see and understand this are the ones who possess power.

Crossing these lines, breaking our physical and our emotional limits, is the most difficult thing to do, but also the most beautiful. It causes pain on many levels, it causes blood to spill all over the place

39

and our hearts to break in pieces. We have to take down that wall with our bare hands. Our knuckles bleed, we are sweating and our whole bodies hurt. We want to give up, we want to go back home, collapse and forget about everything. We may feel that others are better than us, despite the fact that they don't work as much as we do. Everyone hurts on their way to success. Maybe we're wired that way, because otherwise we wouldn't feel real. And after we manage to do all this and we break that wall, we understand. Success is waiting for us on the other side.

At first, I didn't even know what I was doing. That stuffed gym, with so many people trying their luck. The worn wooden floor and the hard punching bags. The old vests and the big helmets. Our bare feet walking on the rough floorboards and hitting the sand-filled bags, which were ending up like a rock at the bottom and almost empty at the top. However weird it might sound, these are some of my best memories. I was not too confident, at least not in this field. People around me didn't seem to believe in me much either. But my mom was always there, along with my best friend and my coach.

Remember those times when you were a little kid and you believed in fairy tales? You would just have to close your eyes and boom! – you had utter fate. But at some point, you grow up and you have to open your eyes and look around yourself. And you see that the real world is a bit different than the way you thought. This may hold you in place for a while; the fact that you are not a princess and no Prince Charming will come riding on a white horse to save you. You are all by yourself and you realize that you have to learn how to do things on your own. You can stay away from all of this, or you can fight. And I know one thing: losing is a million times better than never trying.

This is exactly how it was when I was told about a national competition. The first time, I preferred to stay away. But not the second time. I remember that moment as if it was yesterday. I was afraid. I couldn't think and my whole body refused to listen to me. And I lost. And the same thing happened the next time.

There is a time in our lives when we feel like saying 'Enough!' We feel like shouting it out loud and making people see that it is over, because we work too hard and nothing seems to come of it. We can't say why we should go on, but we can easily say why we want to give up. We can quit any time, but can we leave the playing field so easily?

The National Championship came too soon. My coach put me in and told me that he believed in me. I smiled up at him, but I already felt like I stood no chance. I stepped on the colorful floor mat and he gave me a thumbs up. He was a nice, kind man. He acted the same with the champions and the ordinary people who stepped in his gym. That match would be the one to change my perception on everything. After the first round, my opponent was three points ahead; after the second one, she had four. I sighed as I sat down on the chair and looked up at the man who had taken care of me like a second father. He started explaining strategies to me, but his words were disappearing in the distance, as a familiar song started playing. There was a lot of noise, but in that moment, the only thing I could hear was that song.

> *Here we go, it's getting close;*
> *Now it's just who wants it most.*
> *It's just life, that's how it is,*
> *Cause we have our strengths and weaknesses.*
> *I have visions, can't you see,*
> *I'm on the move, make way for me.*

My coach's voice brought me back to reality. He told me what I had to do, but I had no idea what he had said. I got up from the chair, shook his hand and went back on the floor. Sweat rolled down my face and my dobok was sticking to my body under the heavy equipment. My heart started racing as the noise came back on and the song disappeared. I don't know what happened after that, apart from winning the match.

A famous athlete once said: "Two victories is something. One victory could be by mistake." I agree with him. After that match, I went on to win the silver medal.

WHY IT MATTERS

by Ryan Priest

So my dad thinks I'm an asshole. He doesn't come right out and say it but it's obvious by the way he rolls his eyes when I try to explain myself. I tell him that it's not about the blood and the violence but he scoffs.

"It's the purest form of competition that exists."

Another eye roll. He thinks a smug smirk is a somehow a valid counterpoint and like an idiot I act as if it is and plead my case even harder. But he's convinced I'm some bloodthirsty psychopath frothing at the mouth for the sight of human carnage.

"You like boxing. Do you only like boxing because you're watching a guy get hit in the face or is there more to it?"

"Maybe I don't like boxing as much anymore either." Now he's just being obtuse. This has become about more than ultimate fighting. Now it's about politics and worldviews and religion and he's just using fighting as the vehicle to get there.

"Hey buddy, I think you need to take your nuts out of your purse and re-evaluate things. There's nothing wrong with boxing or MMA." I tell him. It should be surprising that someone would speak to their dad like that but this is the world we're living in. Also, I'm a thirty-four year old grown ass man and he's heard far worse come out of my mouth.

"See?" He says as if my questioning his masculinity won him the argument. He walks away and I'm kind of sad. He's my dad. Not some metrosexual barista down at the coffee shop.

I realize what it is though. Why he can't see MMA for anything other than modern day gladiatorial combat.

I let it go because he doesn't know that names like Chuck Liddell and Anderson Silva will one day be known by every self-affirmed sports fan. He doesn't see the future coming but I do.

MMA is beyond any language barrier. It exists in some form in every country on Earth, in every civilization that has ever existed. I know it's going to continue to grow because it can't be stopped. It's out there and there's going to be no getting the genie back in the bottle. It's too important.

Tomorrow a football fan is going to be mugged. Some basketball fan with pictures of Air Jordan on her wall will get slapped around by her boyfriend. Tomorrow some bully will pick a fight with an MMA fan and end up having the worst day of his life. Tomorrow rapes, robberies and assaults will be stopped by someone choking the bad guy out. This hero might not even know it but what he did, he only did because of a guy named Royce Gracie. Every real MMA fan knows it's pronounced Hoyce.

Everyday someone's life is saved by mixed martial arts. And I don't mean in a metaphoric "Soccer got me off drugs and changed my life" type trope. No, the very literal "I was going to be killed and doing something I learned from MMA got me out of it alive."

I'm fighting the urge to run my dad down. Chase him out to the garage where he's retreated to re-engage the argument. Make him listen to one of a thousand stories I know about fighters stopping crimes or how a mixed martial arts enthusiast protected him- or herself. It'd be lost on him. He probably thinks football jocks or baseball players with their pudgy guts could do the same.

There's a generational gap between me and the old man. He never dressed in white pajamas as a kid to learn Tae Kwan Do or Karate. He didn't spend his afternoons practicing kicks and punches against invisible enemies. When my dad was a kid Kung Fu was just something they did in the movies. Like spaceships or dragon slaying or anything else wholly removed from his day to day reality. If he ever had taken a martial art he'd have at least a little respect for a guy who can kick and punch against a very real and very game opponent.

The cage is the laboratory of the street. You don't have to embarrass yourself in a street fight by trying to use a karate chop because guys like Pat Miletich and the Shamrock brothers actually put their bodies on the line to prove that shit was fake.

I'll be honest, a lot of jazz just sounds like noise to me. I don't get, understand or particularly like modern art. Gourmet food tastes like someone took my dinner and poured garden dirt on it. I just don't have the framework to appreciate these things. So I can't blame my dad or anyone else for watching a fight and seeing only a mess of blood and violence. They simply lack the framework.

But if they did have it and saw fighting through my eyes they would see that the violence is really a beautiful and articulate symphony of movement. I don't even see the blood. I only see a substance that can blind a fighter or allow him to slip out of submissions like a greased pig. When my dad sees a guy get knocked out he can't help but cringe and think of it as a garish and altogether unnecessary blood sport. What I see is a man paying the ultimate price to show us all what not to do.

I decide to go into the garage but I don't bring up ultimate fighting. He's working on another one of his cars. This is what he knows about, gears gas and speed. It drives him crazy that I can't even tell the difference between and a Honda and a Toyota. I'm sure he thinks the subtle differences are important.

I help him when he asks me to hand him tools. I pay attention and try to follow what he tells me about these old cars. It's okay if I don't take it all in. It's enough that he wants to share something he loves with me.

Tomorrow Pearson fights Sotiropoulos. Maybe I'll come back over with a few beers and just maybe I'll be able to get him to tell a triangle from an armbar. Even if he can't understand why the difference between the two is so important.

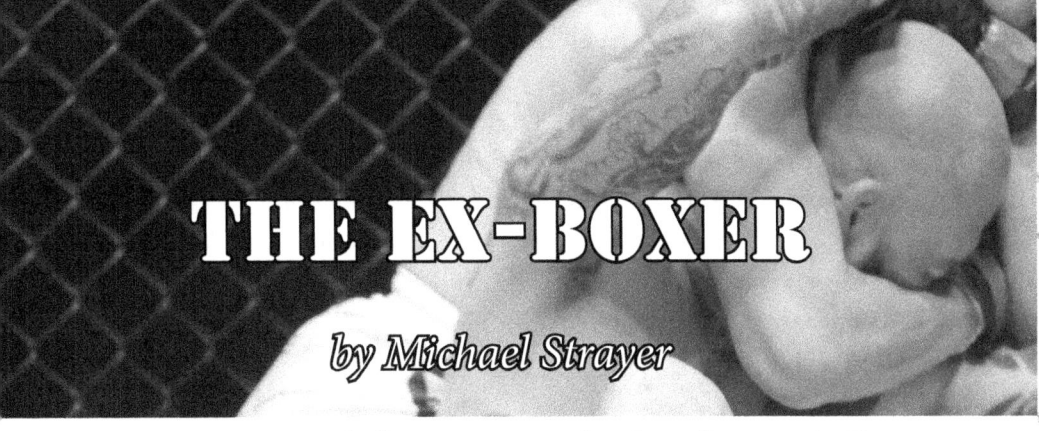

THE EX-BOXER

by Michael Strayer

Autumn arrived all at once on an October afternoon in Kacey, California. Leaves the color of fire, billowing and rolling like fire, twisted down Main Street as the ex-boxer walked, duffel slung about his shoulders, wearing a tattered pea-coat, a weathered beanie, once gray now black as bruised skin. He paused for a moment and watched the leaves. A passing truck sent them roiling in an explosion of yellows, oranges, and reds. The ex-boxer went on.

His name was Oliver. He stood six-nine, as wide as an icebox—in his time, Oliver had been a heavyweight. Boxing gloves, jump ropes, hand wraps, and mouth-guards padded mutely against one another inside the duffel, their weight on his shoulders like the comforting hands of a trusted friend. He passed the old theatre, abandoned now, its marquee empty but for a lone "**L**," and turned right up Fifth Street. The leaves scampered after him.

Fifth was darker than Main; the buildings tall and imposing; casting big blue shadows; covered in layers of graffiti; the trees bereft of adornment and skeletal. Oliver bid good day to a couple of bums, puttering for cans in an alleyway.

"Afternoon Champ," said one. "Goin' to Mike's?"

"You know it."

The ex-boxer smiled and kept walking. The bums returned to their scavenging.

Oliver had once been great. Or close to it. In Kacey, he was a legend. His first five fights had ended with his opponents sleeping on the canvas, their hopes and dreams of pugilistic stardom dribbling out their noses, lips and eyebrows in scarlet streams. Oliver was going to be big—everyone knew it: A heavyweight slugger with the kind of Mike Tyson potential that drove fans to screaming. He was

47

going to be Kacey's salvation; the town's ticket out of ambiguous Americana and into the light of national recognition. And then, one day, inexplicably, Oliver quit. He'd continued training, but had never fought again. He was still respected, of course, still called Champ by some, sometimes even shown a glimmer of admiration—but no more than you'd expend on a war vet who'd come home crippled, or a bankrupt billionaire.

The buildings and structures of Fifth Street grew dirtier as Oliver walked. Pale, cadaverous faces peered out filth-streaked windows. Garbage on the sidewalks. Gang emblems labeling doors. A smell of staleness and vomit and depredation. Fifth Street, in contrast to Main, was known as the dangerous section of Kacey. Teeming with violent youth, bandits, and whores. Here, the outcasts resided and, if possible, they were avoided. If there was a murder in Kacey (a rare occurrence, but an occurrence nonetheless) the body was inevitably found beaten, robbed, and straddling a dark corner on Fifth. Oliver walked nonchalantly, indifferent to the danger surrounding him. Eyes shone in his direction from out of alleyways like wolf's eyes in a haunted forest. Bums. Gnarled. Harmless. The vagabond damned. They would enjoy the pleasantry of a Kacey fall for a month or two more and then, with the onset of winter, they'd leave for southern lands, leaving nothing behind; grimy, misbegotten ghosts.

At the end of Fifth Street leered Iron Works Gym (Mike's colloquially, named for its troll-like owner); a metal warehouse between the street and the roaring freeway beyond. It gleamed hotly in the late light. In fading letters the name **Iron Works** was painted over the entrance. A cartoon dumbbell beside it. As Oliver neared the building, he could hear faint sounds emanating from within— music, the bird-chirp chime of a bell. Sounds as familiar as his own heartbeat.

The ex-boxer walked up the front steps and went inside. He was met with a variety of smells, faces, and greetings.

" 'Sup Champ," someone shouted.

"Ollie! It's been awhile!" another.

"Yo, sparring today?"

Oliver's was an increasingly infrequent visage at Mike's. He waved and unshouldered the duffel. He surveyed the gym, slowly, like a draught of good scotch. Two kids in the boxing ring, wearing headgear. Bloody gloves. The rhythmic *Whump! Whump! Whump!* of leather-bound fists colliding into tape-covered heavybags. A rat-a-tat-tat machine gun noise of speed bags bouncing under rolling knuckles. The place smelled of stale sweat and rust. Moldering leather. Ancient and blood-spotted canvas. In three minute intervals, with a minute between rounds, a bell sang. Mike's was a strange and ceaseless cacophony of sounds—heavybags teetering; men grunting; trainers yelling; hip-hop music; the hum of the speed bags; the whisper of swishing jump ropes. And the bell; always the bell; ringing, endlessly ringing—the most important sound in all Creation.

Oliver bent and delved into his duffel and removed two lengths of fetid fabric and began to wrap his hands. His movements were slow and methodical. Almost a reverence to them. Over, around, through the fingers. Repeat. Like a monk fiddling prayer beads, or a supplicant speaking the rosary. He could still remember the first time he'd wrapped those hands; how difficult it had been, how clumsy he once was. The wrap had come loose and unraveled itself just minutes later as Mike coached him through his first shadowboxing session. The cotton had dangled from his wrists in ribbons and he'd looked a kind of recently revived mummy.

He smirked to himself as he finished. A snug fit. Not too tight, not loose. Perfect.

A shadow draped across his arms, and two legs materialized before him; denim covered legs and dirty and with patches of pale skin shining through periodic tears and holes. A pair of shoes. Grimy Nikes. "Good afternoon Ollie," a gruff voice drifted from above. There was an odor to the shoes, moldy and rancid.

Oliver straightened, towering over the man. The legs melted into a round belly, belly into barrel chest, chest into thick neck and tiny head. A bald patch amongst the wisps of red hair gazed at the ex-boxer like a blind eye.

"Hey Mike." He took the pro-offered hand in his. Powerful grip. Made to crush things. They released. "How's it going?"

"It's goin'," said Mike. He had to strain his neck to meet

Oliver's eyes. Myriad warts swathed over his face caught the fluorescent lighting overhead and flared. "Wadda we got goin' on today?"

Mike O'Hara. Proud founder of Iron Works Gymnasium. An old-school brawler from the cobbled streets of Dublin. He hadn't been quite good enough. Always a contender, never a champion. After a series of bloody losses he'd come to America, and had settled in Kacey shortly after. He now lived alone and impoverished in a tiny decrepit studio above the gym, and he ate, slept, and shit boxing.

Once, Oliver had called him Coach.

"Oh, you know," he said. "The usual. Just the basics."

Mike's eyes lit up. He beheld the ex-boxer, his ex-pupil. They rarely saw each other anymore. "The basics huh? That's nice... Say how'd ya' feel about given us a workout, like old times?"

Oliver studied his former coach. He seemed a semblance of himself. Rheumy and trembling. A punchy slur. Poor dumb bastard. No one had taken it harder when Oliver quit boxing than Mike. It was like all hope he'd ever had of seeing a championship belt had vanished, then. Oliver had been his last chance, his fountain of youth, and when he'd left, the floodgates had opened and the eroding tides of Time had begun to consume Mike with rapacious speed. It had only been a few years and already Mike looked twice the age. Oliver sighed, shook his head.

"Sorry coach. I'm just trying to get a sweat on today... Maybe some other time."

A frown lanced across Mike's face and for a moment he looked like he was going to cry, and then the moment passed and his face was an impassive mask of scars, warts and abrasions once again.

"Okay," he said. "Okay. Some other time. Have a good workout."

Mike turned and walked away.

Oliver felt a pang of guilt, watching Mike go. *Maybe I should let him work with me*, he thought. *Couldn't hurt any...*

But no. Oliver didn't want to train with Mike, not anymore. He didn't share Mike's nostalgia for the Old Times. He'd left those behind, now, for better or worse.

Mike disappeared up the shadows of a stairwell, and Oliver went to his workout.

It was a simple routine. He started with shadowboxing. Standing in front of a mirror, bobbing and weaving. Slipping make-believe punches. Hurling volleys of lightning jabs and crosses. Next, jump rope. The metronomic whipping of the plastic cord upon the floor—*whick whick whick*—induced in him a trancelike state. *Whick whick whick.* He had only his breath, and the swinging vault of rope, and his burning calves. The ringing bell. Tolling away the hours. *Whick whick whick.*

After jump rope came bag work. Oliver squared off with a dangling heavybag, dented and misshapen and pieced together with silver stitches of duct-tape.

Ding-ding went the bell.

He began to box.

He launched a powerful left hook to the midsection of the bag. In his mind he saw an opponent cringe, knuckle digging into rib—felt the tremor of resistance undulate up his arm and into his chest and the bag pirouetted away. Came back. Was met with a straight right. Wobbled backwards, the rusty chains clanging notes of protest. His sweat flung in nebulous starbursts. Air hissed between his teeth in time with his attacks. Round after round, he fought, and, fighting, he thought about his life, his forfeited greatness. When he'd quit, people had wanted to know why. They'd needed answers. Oliver hadn't been able to supply a reason; still couldn't. There'd been speculation of injury—of trauma of some sort, perhaps, of pressure, or cowardice—but there'd been none. The simple truth was that Oliver didn't have a reason. He'd searched and searched, traversed his very soul, and no plausible explanation had ever arisen from the mists of uncertainty.

The bell clamored and the ex-boxer's hands fell to his sides. Droplets of sweat dotted the floor and the bag creaked, swaying to eventual motionlessness. He breathed, slowly, in and out, and a cramp in his side let go its claws. He shook out his arms, danced on the balls of his feet.

Ding ding.

He could remember the day it happened, the day he'd quit. He'd been training—sparring—and the bell had rung and as abruptly as wind leaving a bird's wings, the desire to fight had left him. It had been a strange experience. Almost visceral, a tangible sensation of loss; of losing. Like a priest who'd abandoned his faith to the cosmos, Oliver had no longer wanted to fight. *His* God had forsaken him. And just like that, he'd stopped. He'd kept training, but his days of competitive boxing had ended. He was yet haunted by the suddenness of it, how quickly things could change, still fumbling for answers in the dark.

The ex-boxer moved through his workout and outside the sun sank. Dusk darkened into night and a crooked moon rose and smiled down on Kacey like some great jester in the sky. One by one the denizens of Iron Works vacated the gym until only Oliver remained, hammering away at a heavybag. His body steamed in the cold. His grunts of effort carried on the autumnal breeze, into the parking lot. The bell gave a final cry. Its high-pitched voice lingered in the ensuing silence.

Oliver felt his neck hairs prickle. He turned. Staring at him, obscured in the lightless gloom of the staircase, was Mike, his face sad, resentful, and confused.

"How long have you been watching?"

"Long enough," said Mike.

Oliver said nothing. They ogled each other, silently.

"Why did you quit? Give us the truth, now."

Oliver did not reply. Mike fixed him a last, baleful glance and then, wordlessly, went back up the stairs.

The ex-boxer waited. "I wish I knew, coach," he said, finally, to no one, "I wish I knew."

Pale moonlight bathed Fifth Street as Oliver walked. The buildings were dark, silhouetted by the moon, and like the ogres of a child's nightmares. The street was quiet but for the dry rattling of leaves and the scuff of Oliver's shoes on the concrete. The houses, for the most part, were dark, though now and again the ex-boxer spied families sitting down for dinner. The stars winked above and airplanes traveled in slow-moving progression between the stars across the firmament and the air was brisk and the evening about as tranquil as they come.

Then:

"Help!"

"Shut up bitch."

"Hellppp meeee!"

This, followed by a scream—a howling shriek of sinus-wrenching pitch. The sounds of a struggle. Garbage rolling. Glass breaking. Another scream.

Oliver paused, looked about for the source of the noise. Dead trees... Empty buildings... Scurrying leaves... Dark alleyways... He squinted suddenly.

At the end of an alley, illuminated by the white glare of a streetlamp, was a group of three men. Like vultures around a carcass they loomed in a semi-circle over a girl. Her right eye was purple and swollen and her cheeks red and lips split and she was crying; crying and trying to scoot away, away into the protective darkness.

One of the men—tall, skinny, sneering—reached out and grabbed the girl by a lock of her long blonde hair and yanked her to her feet. The girl yelped in pain and screamed. Another of the group slapped her, hard (Oliver could hear the fleshy Whap!), and oblong flecks of blood spattered into the air, jewel-like under the light. Two of the thugs seized the girl by her arms and the third tore down her shirt and she wore no bra beneath the shirt and the group cheered and the girl wept helplessly.

Oliver had seen enough.

He charged down the alley, cocking back his fists. When he reached the group he loosed a savage cry and the girl's aggressors—stunned—let her go. The ex-boxer didn't think. Instinct took over. He smashed his fist into the nearest one's face and there was a crunch under his knuckles like gravel beneath a shovel and a torrent of blood sprayed and the man collapsed bleeding to his ass.

The other two, prior rendered frozen by the unexpectedness of interruption, speedily recovered. They attacked Oliver at the same time. The ex-boxer ducked a punch, absorbed a kick. Countered. Adrenaline seared through his veins, burned away distractions. Time seemed to slow. A surreal calm washed over him. The girl seized the opportunity and fled and dissipated into the night.

The ex-boxer fought. Punching, dodging, getting punched. Going on. He fought. Flicking his fists with blinding speed. Backing down his opponents. Feeling a long dead emotion begin to resurface. How long had it been, since his last fight? Oh, how he'd missed it! He slipped a jab, rocked on his heels, retaliated. His knuckles bled and his lungs roared and his was face puffy and bruised, and he was smiling. A clean left hook knocked one of the thugs to the ground and Oliver rounded on his sole foe, remembering the thrill of battle. *I'd forgotten*, he thought, advancing on the man. Thinking: *How could I have forgotten? Oh how much I need this how much I love it…* He raised his fists. The man turned to run. *I can't believe I let this go, I can't believe it, tomorrow I start again, just as soon as I'm done here I'm calling Mike and apologizing I'm gonna fight again! I love this I'm getting back in the game I love this—*

Oliver was dead before his mind could register the sound of gunfire. He crumpled to the ground and his brains arrowed of his skull and splattered atop the asphalt. The first thug he'd struck stood over his corpse, nose jagged, broken, face bent in a scowl and dripping. The gun smoked in his hand. The man unloaded his remaining bullets into Oliver's massive cadaver. He spat. Then, he gathered the other two and they limped off into the murk of Fifth Street.

Absolute quiet once more. Leaves tumbled tentatively. One stuck in the gathering blood about Oliver's head. Somewhere, a police siren struck up a lonely wail.

The thugs hadn't looked, but had they leaned a little closer and examined the ex-boxer's face they would have seen that he was smiling. He was smiling, and his expression was one of incredible contentment, as if he'd discovered the secret of the world.

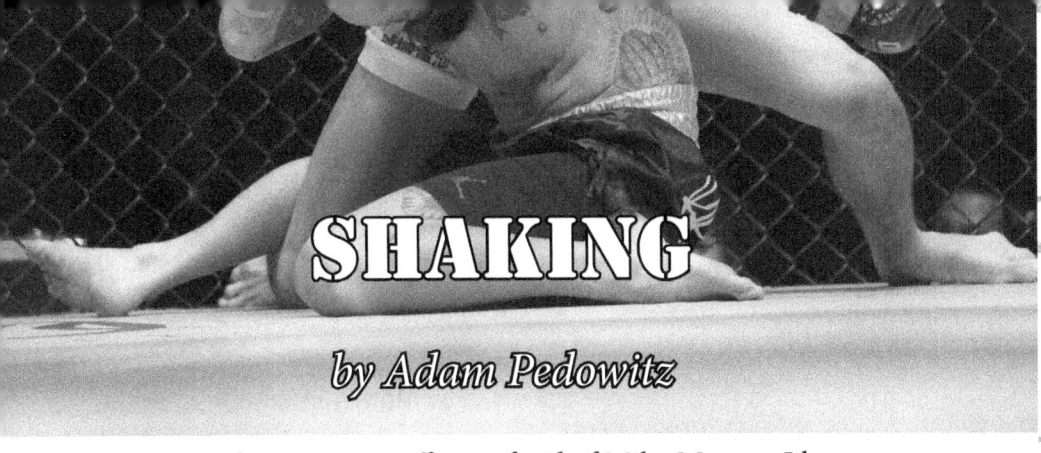

SHAKING

by Adam Pedowitz

Even the training staff was afraid of Mike Marcus. I knew he didn't like me. I was sure of it but I took the open door as an invitation.

To save money, Marcus crashed in a one-bedroom apartment with three other fighters from the gym. I needed a boost. My plan was to ask him nicely for any leftover anabolics. My fight game was dragging. My body was mush. After sparring sessions, I couldn't even hold a cup of water to my mouth. Forget about two-a-days. Forget about the weight cut.

I waited on the sofa, its springs ringing as I sat down. Orange cans of energy drinks were scattered across the floor, as if stacked in a pyramid and then slapped down from the bottom. I thought everyone was gone and felt that familiar loneliness of being strange and yet still unnoticed. But, then again, there was moaning coming from the bathroom to my left.

Marcus had been in the bedroom. He walked out and recognized me without flinching. He was dark, Doberman dark, with a shiny smooth skull. Sweat beaded high on his temples and glittered like a fever. He wore his gym clothes still, with white knee socks and flip-flops. The socks glowed against his skin.

Behind the bathroom door, metal curtain rings scraped against a shower rod. A sharp complaint and the moaning stopped.

"Bathroom's taken," I said, smiling dumbly, knowing my smile was dumb.

Marcus reached a hooked finger into his lower lip and flicked a turd of tobacco against the wall. It thudded and broke apart like a dirt bomb. Brown juice leaked from the corner of his mouth into a plastic cup.

"Yuri's not doing too good," he said. "He probably punctured a lung."

"He did that all by himself?" I said.

"Fuck that guy. It's not something I planned on doing when I got up this morning."

I suddenly heard the thin whispers of Yuri's breathing, distinguished from the rasping air conditioner. In a high school wrestling match I'd made those sounds when my shoulder slipped out of socket. Each breath making the separation worse, feeling that I might puke on the trainer. That was two years ago.

My whole body twitched when I heard the shower turn on. I looked back at Marcus, embarrassed.

"Is he all right?"

"Don't know." Marcus looked over his shoulder and shouted, "You gonna take a shit or get some help?"

"But he's okay."

"I said I don't know. He's in there and I'm out here."

I looked at the door. "You can't get in?"

Marcus pulled the tobacco tin from his pocket and worried the lid with his fingernails.

I walked to the bathroom at the back of the apartment. The bedroom to the right was open and warm and smelled like an old pillow. The door had been taken off the hinges and propped against a wall. I slipped my head inside and saw Fisher on the bed, shirtless, tossing a pink handball to himself with his other hand down his shorts. He looked up without appreciation. Stokley's feet extended from the closet, shin-deep into the room. A bandage covering his torn toenail was soaked through with blood.

"What did Marcus do?"

"Something happened," Fisher told me.

"You don't know?"

"I know it was something."

The bathroom doorknob had a push-lock that could be opened with a screwdriver.

"You never tried to get in?"

Fisher threw his ball at me, and then brought his hands together beneath his shorts. "He locked the door," he said. "What do you think that means?"

From the closet I heard the scrape of a lighter. Smoke began to appear above Stokely's feet and the room's scent sweetened, like a weed sauna. I found this acceptable.

Then Marcus was behind me, tapping my arm with a vial of clear liquid. The label had been rubbed off.

"See if he wants this."

"What if he doesn't?" I asked.

Fisher yelled at me. "Why are you here?"

I put the vial in my pocket knowing it would stay there. There was a toenail clipper on a bookshelf. I grabbed it. "I'm coming in," I said, louder than I needed to, and popped the lock with the collapsible file. Mostly out of fear I closed the door behind me. No one else tried to get in.

Yuri lay in the tub facing the cream tiled wall, naked but for his hands covering a portion of torso. Patches of wet, blond hairs stuck to his nipples. There was no blood. I thought there'd be blood.

Water splashed off Yuri's body into my mouth, tasting of rust. I adjusted the shower stream.

"Are you dying?" I asked.

His Adam's apple bobbed as though struggling to float in choppy waters. I saw what looked like a car crash in Yuri's side. Not a dent so much, just the purple and yellow shading made it look that way.

With three fingers in his mouth, Yuri said, "I coughed," and then he smeared a wad of bloody saliva on the shower tiles. I somehow felt better seeing the blood.

It was a hard time taking Yuri out to my car. He fell from my arms. I dropped him. Just once.

Outside I saw Marcus already behind the wheel, starting the car. I'd left the keys in the ignition.

"I'm driving," he said through the window.

"You serious?" I looked to Stokely standing in the apartment doorway. "What about you?" I asked.

Stokely's skin was waxy. "I'm so fucked, man," he said. It appeared so. He was looking straight at me but his nose was pointing left.

I got in the backseat with Yuri, his skin slipping across the maroon vinyl. I put his head on my lap and felt it might work out for the best that he and Marcus have some separation.

"I never drive anymore," Marcus said over his shoulder. "All I do is train for that title shot."

"We should go," I said.

"He's not getting any worse. He's smiling."

"You're seeing him upside-down."

Marcus accelerated like we were fleeing an accident, not taking one with us. I was forced to cradle Yuri's head with my hips in a way that struck me as improper. The shocks on my car were shot.

"We're in an emergency. This is emergency circumstances and that means everyone can get out of my way," Marcus said.

Marcus was thirty-two and running out of chances to make it in mixed martial arts. Next month he was scheduled to fight a Brazilian Jiu-Jitsu stud, and with a win he'd have a legitimate case for a title shot, or at least be thought of as a top contender. He'd lose that fight with a dislocated elbow, never get his title shot. No one ever thought of him as a contender, but in the car it felt good to be part of something with Marcus. We were colluding. Word might get out about how I helped save Yuri, I thought. That could be a big deal. I might even get some respect around the gym.

We streaked across the crumbling Jersey City streets, bits of asphalt pinging the chassis like kettle corn. Around us the city was dying and already dead in some places. Brownstones like the one I'd grown up in had been tossed away, stone-by-stone, in huge metal dumpsters, leaving empty lots like missing teeth. No one thought them worth replacing.

Marcus asked me, "You grow up around here?"

58

"We're close," I told him.

Yuri stared up from my lap with something that looked a lot like love. There wasn't blood in his drool anymore. I took that for a good sign.

"You definitely from here," Marcus said, his voice thick. "Nobody knows the streets of this place unless they born by it. Just like every place. I'm from nowhere, know what I mean? I grew up on the streets since I was eight, but for some reason I got no directions. That figures, right? I got nothing in my head that tells me where to go. I just go and somehow I always get to where I need to be. And if I don't? If I get someplace else? Well guess what, that's the place I need to be. I mean, really need to be. Know what I mean?"

I thought I knew. I wanted to.

Marcus put in one of the CDs I kept on the passenger seat and I noticed how different it sounded from the backseat, being driven. To the music, there was a dance happening outside my window that I couldn't figure out, but it was something: the streetlamps, the metal fences catching pieces of paper off the wind, the stumbling people with no place else to be. It was all solid and hard, but it moved.

"Take a left," I said.

"You definitely from around here."

"Left! Left!"

I arched my body into the turn so Yuri wouldn't fall off my lap. After that, Marcus stopped talking for a while. He skipped to the next song on the CD, which I didn't know. It sounded a lot like rejection.

As in most of the cities I've been to, the neighborhood got worse closer to the hospital. Tired men and women on the sidewalks seemed to fall past our car. But they fought forward, or maybe it only appeared so as we slowed down.

"They got a McDonald's at this hospital," said Marcus, suddenly excited.

"Doctors too," I said. "Don't park. Pull up to the front."

But Marcus drove to the back of the lot and stopped next to a bus, parking in its shadow. He turned to look at Yuri. "Tell the doctors you got jumped."

"I think he's in shock," I said.

"Like, four of five dudes beat you down and took your shoes."

"He's fucking bare-assed!"

I felt Yuri's head getting denser, the blood pooling there and turning to sand. His body relaxed but the veins in his neck and chest bulged like blue earthworms. Looking at them made my own neck ache.

"So maybe they took his clothes too. And they could have raped him or something."

"Doctors can tell about that stuff," I said, thinking it was probably true.

"Yeah," Yuri said. It felt like the words were coming from my stomach. "Yeah, yeah, yeah, yeah."

Marcus got out and opened my door. I tried to get out but he put a hand on my shoulder, smelling sweet and rotten with mint tobacco juice. Marcus slammed his fist into Yuri's face while I waited. Some blows glanced off the side of his head and deadened my legs, but I didn't want to show that I felt it. I didn't want to speak. I convinced myself that he knew what had to be done. He was Mike Marcus, for Christ sakes. I was just a kid.

The back of Yuri's head pounded into my balls.

Afterward, we rolled into the circular drive of the hospital's main entrance. Marcus stopped the car and locked the doors. I could have pulled up on the chrome lock and gotten out, but I caught sight of him in the rearview mirror. Right then, with Yuri's jaw shuddering and seizing at tiny bits of air, my only thought was how I wished I hadn't corrected Marcus when he made that wrong turn.

"If he can't say anything, tell the doctors they took his wallet and gold chains too."

"I don't think Yuri owns any chains."

"They don't know that. Yuri can file with insurance or something."

Marcus unlocked the doors. I carried Yuri into the hospital

lobby and placed him on a recently vacated bed with pale-blue sheets. He didn't even move to cover himself.

This was the hospital where I was born, almost three weeks early and jaundiced. Doctors had me placed under a green lamp for days. In pictures I'm shriveled with a head of black hair and a mask placed over my eyes. I looked like a baby mole, head tilted up to sniff out danger or food.

When they rolled Yuri away I almost didn't notice, but he was the only naked man in the huge lobby of sick and injured people. They were rolling him fast, too, just like on television.

I walked outside and saw that Marcus had gone. Tomorrow I'd find out he sold my car for three hundred dollars, but he kept my CDs and would also start letting me know when his connection came through with the steroids.

Back in the waiting room I took a seat next to a colorless girl with a ball of gauze around her index finger. She was pointing it upward, probably because she'd been told to. I felt the vial in my pocket and tried to figure a plan to steal some needles while checking on Yuri.

After his fight, Marcus would refuse and never receive medical attention for his dislocated elbow, so it never healed right. When the gym finally cut him loose, he traveled around the country fighting at small-time shows and county motorcycle rallies. It was for a two-hundred-dollar purse, I heard, that he took a short-notice fight in Laramie, Wyoming, where he faced another arm-bar submission for which he wouldn't tap. Could you ever imagine a trauma-center doctor taking his arm below the elbow while he was out cold?

I'm still shaking.

THE MIRACLE MAN

by Zach Shephard

I guess I should start with the fight at the fairgrounds, because that was my last match before everything went crazy.

At the sound of the bell I limped to my corner and collapsed onto the stool. Everyone gathered around me like an Indy 500 pit crew, Coach massaging my leg while Piston treated the cut above my eye. Someone squirted water into my mouth, but I was breathing so hard it only made me choke.

I slumped against the cage and closed my eyes. My teammates seemed eager to give me advice, but between the screams of the crowd and the ringing in my skull, only three of their words managed to register: "one more round."

That was it. One more round. If I could push myself for the next three minutes and have my hand raised because of it, I'd finally earn a shot at a professional kickboxing fight—I'd finally be able to scratch that item off my list of life goals, and hang up my gloves for good.

Someone slapped me, killing my daydream. My teammates dragged me to my feet and took my stool away, and suddenly I was alone.

The ref pointed my way and asked if I was ready. I guess I must have nodded, because before I knew it Nightmare was coming at me.

I covered up against the first two shots to the head, leaving me open to the follow-up hook to the body. My counter-right convinced Nightmare to back off and circle to the left, where he knew my bum leg kept me from generating any real power. We took a few seconds to catch our breath, then met again in the cage's center.

Nightmare looked about as tired as I felt, but that didn't stop him from popping me with a jab that reopened the cut he'd made earlier. A warm trickle ran down my face and into my eye, adding partial blindness to my list of problems.

I played defensively and conserved my energy, keeping my hands up while Nightmare threw a few sloppy combinations. After his last shot missed by a mile he backed off to suck some wind, and that's when I decided to take my chance.

I shot forward with a flurry of punches. Nothing significant landed, but the sudden rush was enough to make Nightmare back into the fence, where I clinched his head and started throwing some knees.

The first one hit his body with a solid thud. The second was blocked by a forearm. The third glanced off Nightmare's hip, and before I could throw a fourth he ducked under my arms and slipped out to the side.

As we separated, I turned to face him. At least, that's what they tell me happened.

The next thing I remember was being on my back and trying to figure out how to sit up while someone relieved me of my mouthpiece. I didn't find out until later that Nightmare's hook had blasted me hard enough to shower the judges' table with sweat.

And just like that, it was gone. The victory that might have earned me my first pro fight had slipped through my fingers. Again.

I spent a few days wondering what I was going to do with myself, then finally returned to the gym.

After the match at the fairgrounds, Piston was all that kept me going. He wouldn't let me give up, even when I was convinced I was just a mediocre fighter with a bad leg and worse cardio. He made me keep coming to the gym to train, which is the only reason I was in the alley that night.

But before I get to that story, I want to apologize—again. I never realized fighting would be such a lifestyle change for me. I never realized it would be so easy for a guy competing in small-town, amateur events to lose sight of the important things. But kickboxing ended up being an all-or-nothing thing: it required my full devotion, which is why I wasn't able to give you the time and attention you deserved.

Now that I write it, I realize how stupid it sounds.

If I had it my way, I'd spend another twenty pages trying to explain why I did the things I've done. But I've got something important to tell you, and not a lot of time to do it in. I just wanted to apologize one last time, and to let you know that no matter what, I'll always love you.

With that being said, I bring you the main event of the evening . . .

I'd been back in training for a month the night it happened. My car had broken down a couple of days earlier, so I had to walk home from the gym. My leg was sore and it felt like someone was tightening a vice on my chest every time I tried to breathe, but I figured that was just a part of the game.

I was almost home when I came across them. In the gravel alley between the houses was a group of college guys, maybe five or six years younger than me, enjoying some beers under the moonlight. I kept my head down and cinched up my gym bag on my shoulder, and politely declined when they offered me a drink. I'd almost made it past when one of them recognized me.

"Hey," he said, pointing. "That's the guy who got his ass kicked at the fairgrounds."

They had a good laugh at that, which was fine with me—I would've been perfectly content to keep on walking. Unfortunately, things changed when one of them grabbed my arm.

The thing you have to know about drunken frat boys is that when they see a fighter, they suddenly decide they've got something to prove. It doesn't matter that they're in an alley in a small town's residential area, where anyone glancing out their back window might see what's going on. An opportunity's an opportunity, as far as they're concerned.

I got a good shot in on the first guy: a straight right, right down the middle. It was the strongest punch I could throw with my screwed-up leg, because hooks require a lot of hip-twisting I can't really manage. The night was just dark enough to keep me from hitting the chin for a knockout, but I busted his nose so badly that he backed off screaming, which was just as good.

My knuckles hurt like hell, but I took a swing at the next guy anyway. My gym bag slowed me down, and he covered up just enough to avoid the hit while his buddy clubbed me over the head with a bottle. I'm pretty sure it didn't shatter like they do in the movies.

I was chewing on gravel when they started kicking me. I decided it was easier to just cover up and absorb the hits until they got bored, which didn't take long.

The drunks passed through a backyard gate and returned to their house. If any of the neighbors had seen what had happened, they didn't care enough to do anything about it.

I lay there bleeding, my head throbbing, my ribs screaming. As I faded away, I saw a hole rip into the air before me, like an oval filled with television static. A tall figure stepped through, and that's when things got really weird.

I woke up in the bed of a truck with a cloth draped over my eyes. Wherever I was, I knew there couldn't have been a paved road beneath me, because I wasn't exactly getting a smooth ride. I pulled the cloth from my face, the sun screaming down at me. I sat up, shading my eyes.

As far as I knew, there weren't any deserts around Greymill, which meant whoever had picked me up had taken me an awfully long way from home.

There were a number of mysteries I could have worried about at that point—who was driving, what the hell I was doing in a desert, et cetera—but the most important thing on my mind just then was the thing chasing the truck.

The wall of sand stretched high enough to scrape the sky. I felt like I was staring at an oncoming tidal wave in some big-budget disaster movie. The truck was probably doing forty or fifty miles an hour, but the sandstorm was gaining anyway; it wasn't long before the cloud blotted out the sun and left everything in a golden shadow.

I turned to yell something at my driver, but the truck's window was tinted black and there was a lot of noise out there, so communication wasn't going to happen. Above the window I saw a manufacturer's logo I didn't recognize, and although I'm no car expert, I'm pretty sure none of the big motor companies brand their vehicles with two slash marks and a star inside an oval.

I looked down and realized there was something bulky under a tarp next to me. I took a peek and saw a bunch of equipment I'd expect to find in a secret government lab—you know, the really advanced technology they hide from the public.

That's when I heard the roar. My driver must have heard it too, because he stepped on the gas. I looked behind us and saw something more than just a bunch of dust.

A set of teeth shot out of the sand-cloud, just far enough to show themselves before disappearing again. They were huge and pointy and high off the ground—whatever chased us was big, mean and fast. It was keeping pace with the storm, which was a problem, because we weren't.

The sand closed in, and so did the giant running inside it. I saw the teeth poke out again like a monster coming through a golden portal to hell, and I'm pretty sure I pissed myself when the thing opened its jaws and roared. I guess I'd describe it as a meaner version of a T-rex, but it was hard to get any real details under those conditions—everything was the color of dirty gold, sort of dark but sort of not.

If I was scared before, I was downright terrified when the sand overtook us. It was like falling into a tank of black water when you know there's a shark in there somewhere. Visibility was shit; from where I sat against the cab, I couldn't see anything past the tailgate.

The next roar I heard was so loud that it shook the truck. Even more disturbing than the sound was the hot breath blowing over me.

I only saw the clawed hand for a split-second when it materialized out of the cloud and slapped the side of the truck. I remember being thrown from the bed and rolling, and I'm happy to say I don't remember a damn thing after that.

When I woke up again I was on a long bed—the stationary kind, not the truck kind. The room was hospital white, but something about it was off: the doorway was a foot higher than normal, as were the counters and chairs. The floor seemed awfully far away.

I looked to my left and saw a machine monitoring how much life was left in me. The symbols on the screen weren't any numbers I knew.

I was just about to try sitting up when the door opened. A woman came through with a smile on her face and an electronic tablet in her hands. She looked to be in her late 30s, with a ponytail the color of tree bark.

She introduced herself as Natalie and got right down to business.

"You're a lucky man. Not a lot of people see a sand-kitten up close and live to tell about it."

(The monster wasn't actually called a sand-kitten, but its name was something I could barely pronounce and wouldn't stand a chance of spelling out, so bear with me.)

Natalie climbed into a nearby chair; it was as high as a bar stool.

"Where am I?" I asked.

"A hospital. But not the kind you're used to."

"I don't suppose you could be more specific."

Natalie took a breath, exhaled. "This is going to be a little hard to swallow."

"I was just chased by a five-story sand-kitten through an Arabian desert that apparently exists somewhere in western Washington. Try me."

Natalie smiled at that, though I got the feeling she still wasn't convinced I'd be ready for what she had to say. She ended up being right.

"You got into a fight in an alley recently. Do you remember that?"

"Barely. I blacked out at the end."

"Do you recall what happened just before you lost consciousness?"

I thought back and remembered the oval of TV static that had appeared in the air. When I told her about it, I expected her to think I was nuts, but she treated it like everyday conversation, as if I were talking about a trip to the grocery store.

"It was Javos who picked you up," she said. "He was looking through the Veil and just happened to see you at the right time. He knew he wasn't supposed to step through, but he couldn't help himself—he was afraid you were going to die."

"Okay," I said. "You're going to have to explain most of that."

Natalie set her tablet on the counter. She took a moment to compose her thoughts, then: "You're not exactly on Earth anymore."

I didn't say anything, which she took as a signal to continue.

"The scientists here still aren't exactly sure how it works. It seems as though this place occupies the same space as Earth, but the Veil—a sort of boundary between our dimensions—keeps us separated. Javos was using his equipment to look at the Earth side of things, and when he saw you needed help, he opened a rift—which he wasn't authorized to do—and pulled you through for medical attention."

"And then I got chased and nearly eaten by a sand-kitten."

"Yes, sorry about that. Javos happened to be working in a dangerous area."

It seemed like crazy-talk, but I wasn't going to argue just then. A weird explanation was better than no explanation at all.

As you can probably guess, I had about a hundred questions bouncing through my head at that point. I was just about to ask the first of them when something lit up on Natalie's tablet and drew her attention.

"I need to go," she said, and slid out of her chair.

I tried to sit up, but Natalie would have none of it.

"I know you've been out for a few days, but you should still rest a bit. The surgery took a lot out of you."

"The what?"

Her tablet blinked again. "I'll be back soon."

I called after her, but she seemed pretty set on leaving. In the time she was gone, my hundred questions swelled into a thousand.

Apparently my body agreed with Natalie's advice, because it decided to fall asleep after she left. When I woke up, I found that someone had brought a tray of food to my bedside. I downed two slices of cheese and a healthy serving of fruit, and was just reaching the extent of my appetite when Natalie came back.

"I'm glad you got some rest," she said. "Now—where were we?"

"Surgery," I said. "As in, I've apparently had some."

"Right. Sorry about that. The Terravons don't have the same laws about medical consent that you do on Earth. Complicated surgeries are an everyday thing here."

"Just how complicated are we talking? Tell me I'm not missing any organs."

"No, nothing like that. They just did a full scan of your body and found some things that needed repairing."

Naturally, my thoughts went straight to my leg. I moved it around a bit under the sheet to test the waters. There didn't seem to be any pain, but I wasn't in a good position to do any serious exploring.

"I saw the scans," Natalie said, watching as I flexed my leg in and out. "It looked like you had some pretty bad damage in there. We don't think it was a result of being thrown from the truck, though."

"No, it'd been that way for years. Jiu-jitsu accident."

"Well, you won't have to worry about it anymore. Your leg's in top shape now."

That was certainly something I would have loved to believe, but after being only half a kickboxer for a few years, I had my doubts. I moved my leg around some more, and it gave me a sudden urge to get up and go for a test-jog.

At that point, Natalie went into a few of the details regarding Terravon surgical techniques. I'm not going to spell it all out here (mostly because I didn't understand half of what she said), but the gist of it is this: my leg had essentially been reconstructed with a bunch of strengthening implants. The way she explained it, it sounded like I'd been turned into some sort of cyborg—but when I made that observation, she pointed out that the materials in my leg were virtually identical to human bones and muscles and tendons. I wouldn't be setting off any metal detectors at the airport, and even a trained surgeon wouldn't be able to find anything unusual inside me. Basically, I was the only person who would know anything had changed, and that was only because my leg would be so much stronger than before. There weren't even any scars from the procedure.

I know all of this sounds crazy. Hell, I wouldn't believe it myself if I hadn't seen it with my own eyes. But if you've managed to make it this far without dismissing everything as a messed-up delusion, I hope you'll go just a little bit further. This next part is kind of rough, so you may want to sit down. That's what Natalie did, right before she told me.

"There were a lot of things to fix when we went in for surgery. The damage from the truck accident, the cuts from the alley fight, your leg . . . we patched everything up as best we could, but there was still something beyond our reach."

She picked up her tablet and tapped the screen. She looked up at me and pulled her lips into her mouth, as if that might keep her from having to give me the news.

"You've been having troubles breathing lately, haven't you?"

I shrugged. "My cardio's seen better days."

She nodded, consulting her tablet again. She was obviously trying to stall, but finally decided to turn the screen toward me.

"This is an image of your chest." Her finger looped around the tablet once, gesturing at the whole picture. She then traced a white area in the middle of the shot. "And this is the tumor."

It may have been my imagination, but I'm pretty sure the room got a little darker then.

I'd describe to you how I reacted, but you can probably make a pretty good guess on your own. I really didn't want to tell you like this, but in the end, I think it's better this way. In any case, I should probably go on with the story. I am on the clock, after all.

After giving me the news, I think Natalie may have taken my hand. If she did, I wasn't really aware of it.

"I'm sorry we couldn't remove it," she said. "Cancer is a puzzle even Terravon technology hasn't been able to solve."

I asked her about radiation or chemo, but apparently the cancer was too far progressed for either of those to have much chance of being effective. Natalie said the treatments would just end up making me feel sick for the rest of my days, which wasn't how I wanted to go out.

I'd be lying if I said I didn't do a lot of crying for the rest of the day. Natalie came back and checked on me regularly, but I wasn't much in the mood for company. All I really wanted was to get out of that bed. When you've only got a few months left, the last thing you want to do is lie around all day.

The next morning, Natalie unhooked me from everything and led me outside at my request. Apparently my release was a bit earlier than scheduled, but she wasn't going to fight me on it.

I guess the Terravons were a shy bunch, because I never saw one on the way out of the hospital. Natalie and I exited through the building's back door, which took us to a garden that looked like it belonged outside a palace. We went down a short flight of steps to the trimmed lawn, where we took a walk beside a shallow, football-field-sized pool with an enormous fountain in the middle. There were colorful flowers mixed into the bushes at the borders of the garden, and despite the previous day's news, I found myself calmed by the serenity of it all.

We walked in silence for a long while, the sunrise creeping

over the bushes to splash everything with orange paint. After a time I asked Natalie about her story, because I really wasn't interested in thinking any more about mine.

"Back on Earth I was an archaeologist," she said. "Or I almost was, anyway. I hadn't quite graduated yet, but after another two semesters of getting coffee for my misogynistic professor and transcribing his handwritten notes, I would have finally earned my degree."

"What brought you here?"

"Curiosity. And luck. I got invited to a dig site by a colleague of mine, and when I went off by myself I came across a tear in the Veil. It was a jagged-edged sheet of black and grey snow, similar to what you saw in the alley—except my tear was different, because it was a natural occurrence, rather than a rift made by someone on the other side.

"The whole thing was sort of hypnotic. I probably should have gone back to tell someone what I'd found, but I completely forgot about everything around me. I dipped my hand into the tear and felt a tickle run through my arm. There was no resistance, so I pushed farther. Next thing I knew, I was over here."

"And you decided to stay?"

"Sort of. I made the choice to poke around for a bit, but when I came back to the tear, it had already healed itself."

"So you were stuck?"

Natalie nodded. "I can't say I regret it, though. I love it here. I've been around an awfully long time, and I still haven't learned all there is to know about the Terravons."

We turned the corner of the pool. Somewhere to our right, a flock of birds woke up and started singing like piccolos.

"Do you ever feel like going back?"

"To Earth? Sometimes. Just for a visit, at least. But I can't let myself do it."

"Why not?"

"Because I'm afraid I won't make it back here. Terravon equipment has only figured out how to open rifts on this side of the Veil. If you don't make it back through your rift before the Veil repairs itself, you're stuck on Earth."

I can't be sure, but out of the corner of my eye, I thought I saw her shiver.

"That's my nightmare," she said. "Leaving this place and never finding my way back."

She looked up at me then, her eyes squinting against the sunlight.

"What about you? Are you going to stay?"

I stopped and took in the scenery. The birds kept singing their songs and the fountain kept trickling. I took a deep breath to smell the flowers, but paid for it when I felt a sharp pain in my chest.

"It's a gorgeous place," I said. "But I've got some things I need to take care of back home."

Some of the sun's light seemed to drain out of Natalie's face, and she did a poor job of masking her disappointment with a forced smile. "You've got to do what's right for you," she said.

We finished our trip around the pool. I knew I couldn't afford to waste any time, so I had Natalie arrange for an Earthward rift to be opened that evening.

Everything was set up and ready to go. All Natalie would have to do was push a button and I could step through the static and end up on Earth. The device looked sort of like an old slide projector with some glowing coils attached. Natalie had arranged for my exit point to be the garden, since she'd recognized how much I'd enjoyed the place.

We were the only two there, waiting for the machine to power up as the sun started to set.

"I forgot to ask," Natalie said. "What day was it on Earth, when you left?"

"The twenty-eighth," I said. "September."

"Year?"

"Two-thousand eleven."

She smiled and shook her head.

"What?"

"Nothing. I just didn't realize it had only been that long. I haven't run the numbers in a while."

"You don't have calendars here?"

"We do, but they're not the same as yours. Time flows differently here—just another one of the questions our scientists haven't answered yet. I've been here a little over a decade, but on Earth, time has just been crawling by."

"Wait. So you're saying that when I get back—"

"No one will even know you were gone."

I wasn't sure what I thought about that. I asked myself if the time difference was a blessing or a curse in regards to my cancer, but couldn't figure it out. Either way, I guessed I was only going to be around for a few months, whether those months took place on Earth or anywhere else.

A beam of light shot out of the machine and cut a nice, clean hole into the air about five yards away. I could tell Natalie was going to have some trouble with this goodbye, but I couldn't think of anything I could say that would comfort her, so I let her do the talking.

"Some of your cuts from the fight might open back up when you go through," she said, fighting against her sniffles and keeping her eyes low. "It's just a side-effect of passing through the Veil. Your leg should be fine, though. It's fixed for good."

I took Natalie's hand, because she'd been a big help and it just seemed like the thing to do. She looked up at me, and when the tears broke free and hit her face she lunged in for a hug. I held her there for a moment before the rift flickered and made a weird humming noise. She backed away, wiped her cheeks with the backs of her hands and told me I should go before the thing closed on me. We said our last goodbyes and I left the Terravon world behind me.

I can't say what the experience with the rift was like, because I don't actually remember it. I just remember waking up in the alley where I'd been jumped by the frat boys. It was still dark there, and I think I heard their voices in the nearest yard for a few seconds before they went inside. I tried to move and realized that Natalie had been right—my cuts were reopened and even my bruises felt tender again. There was also a familiar pain in my ribs that I wasn't happy to experience.

I rolled onto my hands and knees and got to my feet. I picked up my gym bag and finished my walk home. If my leg was hurting, I didn't notice.

The next day of training was an interesting one. I went straight from the warehouse to the gym, where Piston was eager to get to work. He asked about my leg, as he always did, and I told him it was feeling good. I didn't tell him why, because I didn't want to look like a lunatic. He held some pads for me and asked what I wanted to start with. I told him I wanted to fire off a few right round kicks—it was time to see how hard that new-and-improved left leg could pivot.

Piston, after failing to find success in the ultra-competitive welterweight division, had recently been bulking up to fight at light-heavyweight. He was a mountain of muscle and looked as strong as ever, which was what made that first kick of mine such a surprise.

My shin hit the pads so hard that his arms snapped back and he punched himself in the face. If you're picturing him knocking himself out, that's an exaggeration—his knuckles just hit his lips enough to wake him up. But still, a guy that strong should have been able to hold the pads for me without having them move an inch.

His eyes showed me that he was as surprised as I was.

"Do that again," he said.

And I did. This time, he was ready for it and didn't punch himself, but that didn't mean my power had dropped at all.

Piston called Coach over to have a look at "the miracle man." I fired off a few more kicks, all as hard as the first. When my shin hit those pads, the slap that carried through the gym was like a crack of thunder.

A crowd gathered at about the time I started doing switch-kicks. After having tested the right leg, I wanted to see how hard I could hit with the left.

Pretty hard, it turns out.

It wasn't just power, though—I had speed, too. The kind of speed I hadn't had since before I got my leg twisted and torn up back in my jiu-jitsu days.

We worked some punches next, focusing mostly on the left hook I hadn't been able to throw in years. There was a time when that had been my best punch, but it's hard to get any power out of it if you've got no snap in your lead leg.

I blasted the pad a few times, much to Coach's delight. It was good to have my punch back.

My leg may have been strong, but my lungs were still getting worked over by a tumor. I was wiped out after ten minutes.

Despite the setbacks, I trained hard for the next few weeks—as hard as I could with my body's screwed-up gas tank, anyway. I asked Coach to get me a fight as soon as he could, and he did.

Second-round TKO.

I beat the hell out of that guy. I was hitting harder than I ever had in my life—even harder than before my injury. Natalie said the Terravon implants wouldn't make me a cyborg, but I was starting to wonder about that. They were giving me a level of strength and speed that I don't think I ever would have had on my own.

Piston had an MMA fight that same night, right after mine. It was the first one at his new weight class. He tossed his man around like a rag doll, got him to the ground and pounded him out. First-round TKO. He looked like a monster at light-heavyweight. We celebrated.

It was good to feel strong in the cage again. I'd won fights since being injured, but I'd never really felt strong. Now, things were different. Things were good.

Still, somewhere in the back of my head, I knew the clock was ticking.

I had Coach sign me up for another fight two weeks later. Normally you want to take more rest time than that, but time wasn't a luxury I had. I wanted to earn that pro fight. It was more important to me than it had ever been before, because I knew things were going to come down to the wire.

I ended that next fight in the first round. My guy came out swinging and tried to blast me with a straight right, but I slipped to the side, stepped forward, and twisted so hard into a left hook that he didn't wake up until half a minute after he'd been counted out.

I was having a good run, so I fought again.

And again.

I won every time, but I could always feel the cancer working away at me. It was getting harder and harder to train at the gym, let alone fight in a cage against someone who wanted his hand raised just as badly as I did. Coach told me I should take a break, but I said that all I wanted was my pro fight, and that I'd gladly rest after I got it. He offered to make a deal with a promoter and call in a few favors to get me on the pro card, but I declined. I wanted to earn that fight, not weasel my way into it. The whole point was in proving that I was capable—that I was strong enough.

So I got another amateur fight and won it, even though I woke up every morning with a coughing fit and went to bed every night sweating like it was the middle of July.

After that last knockout, we got the call. A promoter had been watching me and couldn't deny that my streak looked awfully good. He made me an offer that would scratch an item off my list of life goals.

That in itself may seem like good news, but it gets better: Piston got signed for a pro fight on the same card. Someone had recognized his talent back when he was in the welterweight division, and after seeing his huge improvements in the move to light-heavyweight, they offered him a paid bout. We were both moving up at the same time, which was more than I could have asked for. I went over to his apartment to celebrate, but I showed up a bit early, and that's how I caught him in the act.

He'd been juicing.

I didn't know what to think. I was confused, I was mad, but more than anything, I was disappointed. We'd both worked so hard to get where we were, and now I was finding out those thirty extra pounds of muscle he'd gained had come from steroids. He'd cheated his way into a pro fight.

And that's when I realized the similarities: here I was, bitching Piston out for using performance-enhancing drugs, while some alien cyborg technology was helping me kick people's heads off.

It wasn't fair. The Terravon implants were skyrocketing me to the top, but they weren't even giving me a chance of getting there on my own. It wasn't like I could just shut off my upgrades.

I decided not to rat Piston out, for two reasons: one, I felt that he should man up and turn himself in, and two, I didn't have a lot of room to talk, given my situation. Especially since I'd decided to take my pro fight anyway.

I justified it by telling myself that it wasn't just the leg that was winning fights. My technique was sharp and I was training as hard as a guy with cancer could. The implants helped, sure. But they weren't carrying me the whole way.

The morning of the event, I coughed up something black into my sink. I ignored it, because what else could I do at that point?

Piston and I showed up at the venue early. Our conversations were short and awkward, because neither of us wanted to mention the S-word.

Before we knew it, it was game time—the amateur fights were over and the pro card was about to begin. Piston went to the cage first.

If he was nervous, you never would have known it. He came out aggressive and went straight for the takedown, which he landed. After a little technical maneuvering—and a lot of brute force—he ended up getting his opponent pinned against the cage, on his seat. Piston shot up to his feet, held the guy in place with one hand and blasted him with some nasty rights. His fist popped in and out so fast that no one would ever need to question where his nickname had come from.

The first few shots didn't land cleanly, but when one finally did, it was enough for a knockout. Piston's guy went limp, but

Piston didn't stop there. It's an accepted rule in MMA that you don't stop until the ref stops you, even if your opponent is clearly out cold. This is because even when you think you've got a guy beaten, there's a chance that letting up on your attack might give him an opportunity to recover. If that happens, the next thing you know, you're the one with a face full of canvas. So the best course of action is to wait until the referee stops the fight, because that's when you can be certain it's over.

Because of this, Piston ended up punching an unconscious man in the face four times at full strength. The ref was slow in getting there.

Piston roared and flexed like hyped-up fighters often do after a dominating victory. The fans cheered as he showed them his juiced-up muscles, the veins on his biceps bulging like earthworms under the skin. Piston's dream had finally come true, and he was loving every second of it. He didn't even seem to realize his opponent was still out until the stretcher came into the cage.

It was the type of thing that will quiet even an MMA crowd. No one wants to see a fighter get seriously injured. Piston's excitement died and was replaced by sudden guilt; I could see it in his eyes.

The crowd watched silently as the injured fighter was carried out of the cage. There was a short delay in the event, but after that, things got started again. The show must go on, I guess.

There was one more fight before mine. I spent my last bit of free time in the locker room, warming up on some pads. Every time I kicked and let loose with my full power, I thought about the guy Piston and his steroids had knocked silly. It didn't seem fair. It didn't seem right.

Before I knew it, my opponent was making his way to the cage. Once he was there, his entrance music cut out and mine started up.

"This is it," Coach said. "Your big day. I'm proud of you." He slapped a hand on each of my shoulders and got ready to walk out behind me.

My feet didn't move.

Coach was saying something to me, but I didn't really hear it. All I could think about was what a mess this whole thing was. The goal had been to earn a pro fight, but I hadn't done that. If anyone had earned that fight, it was some Terravon doctors on the other side of the Veil. I was just a cheater who was going to get an innocent guy hurt.

My music ended, so they played it again. Coach asked what the hell was wrong with me.

I didn't answer.

I turned and ran.

When I got home, I turned off my phone and did a lot of thinking.

That was last night.

I spent a lot of years training to be a fighter. It wasn't always easy—hell, it was never easy—but it was what I wanted to do. I committed to it completely, and that meant I had to let go of a lot of other things in life.

And now here I am, with nothing to show for it.

You know, I always hoped we'd get back together some day. Maybe in a few years when I wouldn't be able to fight anymore, and could afford the time and attention it takes to settle down. But I guess I sort of blew that, didn't I?

In the end, it was Natalie who really opened my eyes. She'd spent a decade in another dimension, learning about a strange new race of people, because the pursuit of knowledge was her passion. It was what she wanted to do.

Then, one day, another human came by and changed everything. She was a mess when I left, even though she'd only known me for so short a time. She didn't even get a chance to find out whether or not she liked me, but she couldn't stand to see me go, because connecting with another person is something you can't really put a price on. We just don't realize how valuable it is until it's gone.

I screwed up when I let you go. I still think our passions in life are important—whether they be archaeology, kickboxing or anything in between—but so are the people. There should have been a way for me to work on both. I could have tried harder. I could have made time. I could have done a lot of things, but I guess none of it matters now, because it's too late to make any changes. Passions and people: I've missed my chance with both.

I'm not feeling too well today, both emotionally and physically. I thought about heading to the doctor, but if the Terravons thought I was a lost cause, I don't see how humans could do any better. Since I don't have a lot of time left, I've decided to skip the clinic and work on my life-list instead. I've always wanted to visit Brazil, and this seemed like as good an opportunity as any. I charged a one-way ticket to my credit card, and I'll be leaving for the airport in a few hours. Maybe I'll have time to make it over to Curitiba and visit the Chute Boxe Academy.

Oh, and one last thing: Natalie wanted me to pass a note on to her professor at the university, but I e-mailed him a few weeks ago and he said he didn't know anyone by that name. I figure it's been a decade since he saw her, so maybe he just doesn't remember her. Anyway, I didn't have a chance to put more effort into getting the message across, but if you've got a few spare minutes, maybe you could help me keep a promise. Natalie's note is attached, along with the university's contact info.

Thanks for the help, and sorry again for everything. If I could go back in time, I'd do it in a heartbeat.

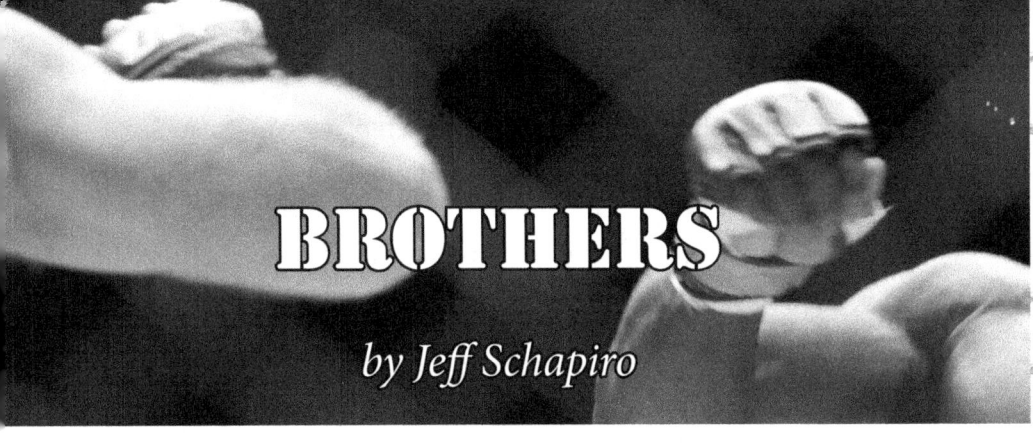

BROTHERS

by Jeff Schapiro

"How's that eye doing, by the way?" Aunt Cindi asked.

"It's fine," I said. "It looks worse than it really is."

I took off my black aviator glasses to show her the damage. She examined it for a moment, holding my chin with her wrinkled hands, turning my head from side to side so she could see it from all angles. Her eyes were full and moist, and with her other hand she fidgeted with the pearls around her neck. She let go of my face and patted my shoulder as she looked away, hiding her tears, and made her way to the coffin.

I looked over at my brother Mike, dressed in his Affliction t-shirt and surrounded by flowers. Inside the casket my mother and I had placed a few of his favorite things: Twizzlers, his white blood-stained boxing gloves, a plush toy monkey from his childhood, and a photo of him with his son in the cage after one of his fights. Those things reminded us of Mike. The funeral home, on the other hand, looked like a floral print tomb, and Mike didn't belong. There was something about his unmoving face that told me he wasn't there anyway.

The answer I gave to questions about the welt on my face became shorter and more ambiguous as the night wore on. Truth be told, I didn't want it to go away. The week before his death we had been sparring inside the barn behind his house, the floor covered in mats so we could train together. We called ourselves stallions, like Rocky, but of German descent. When it came to boxing I usually had the advantage over him, too, but when I got cocky and began to show off – I raised my arms and did the Ali shuffle – he nailed me with a hard jab just before I could get my hands back down to cover my face. That was probably my blood on his gloves, come to think of it.

His little boy, Tristan, who had been playing on the outside stairs with his Ninja Turtles toys, ran into the room and hugged me around the thighs.

"I miss daddy, Uncle Steve," he said softly.

"I know buddy." I squatted so I could speak to him face to face. "We all do."

He began playing with my black silk tie, and asked how long we had to stay there. I looked up at the line, which had grown past the door and out of view, and told him it would be a while longer. He never used to hug me before, but again he threw his arms around me, this time around my neck, and I gave him a squeeze.

"Go play with your toys," I said, fearing my own tears were coming back. "If you want your Game Boy, ask grandma."

The rest of the evening seemed to be a test of patient endurance and manners, and I thought I might run out of either at any time. I was starving, my legs were tired, and there were truly only a few people I cared to share the experience with. Mike lay silently behind me to my right, while my parents and sister stood to my left, weeping on and off throughout the night and graciously accepting the endless number of condolences.

"We're sorry for your loss."

"If there's anything we can do."

"You okay?"

Gray-haired family members I hadn't seen in years poured through the doors alongside close family and friends. They waded their way to the front in their musty gray suits and wrinkled dresses, paid their respects, then left as quickly as possible.

"I'm sorry buddy," said Great Uncle Jack, who I think I met once before puberty. While shaking his wrinkled, arthritic hand, I peered through his thick bifocals. He hadn't been crying.

"Thanks," I said, wondering if he understood just how unfair it was for him to outlive my brother, who just the week before I saw smiling through blood-stained teeth after taking a hit at practice.

After hours upon hours of the same, tedious conversation, our other family showed up, and they were as conspicuous as a missing tooth. They were young and in shape – unusual features in that type of environment – and they were many. Some wore suits, others leather jackets, and still others had donned our fight team's t-shirts. Seth, my training partner, and I locked eyes for a moment. He nodded.

Sporting wrist watches instead of boxing gloves, and sunglasses instead of headgear, they started their journey around the room. Their tattoos were mostly covered. As they approached my family, their tears became more visible, though not all of them were crying. Some stared blankly ahead, while others draped an arm around those who had submitted to their sadness.

Joy and anger – that's all I had known from them before. They were a volatile group. They punched holes in walls when they were angry, and would likely kill someone to protect their families. All of the emotional energy they usually channeled into mixed martial arts suddenly betrayed them and wracked them with sadness.

As the line moved and my teammates drew even closer, I began to wish I had more distant relatives to deal with. The apathetic small talk had become mechanical, and I wasn't yet ready to embrace the heartache that mourning with my team, their embraces, would bring. Tears began to well up again, until suddenly, at the very end of the line, I saw him: Chris Jones, the last opponent Mike had ever fought. He wore a black pinstripe suit and dark sunglasses that covered much of his face, but just a month earlier he was wearing nothing but shorts and MMA gloves, gloating over my brother's unconscious body after knocking Mike out in a local title fight.

"What the hell's he doin' here?" Seth asked as he gathered around me with the rest of the team.

"I don't know man," I said. I hugged each of them and thanked them for coming, embracing each of them for what would have been an uncomfortable amount of time on any other day. We needed each other. But all the while, I couldn't help but peer over their shoulders at the man who, more than anyone, had no business being there.

After the team made their way to the casket together, my mind strayed. I barely noticed anyone standing directly in front of me. What would I say to him? What did he have to say to me? What did he have to say to us? If we were anywhere else, I would tell him what a disrespectful dick he had been to my brother. I would tell him it's a sport and he had no business pulling that shit while the medics were trying to get to Mike.

After he made his way halfway around the room, my mother must have seen him too. She leaned over and muttered, "Um, Honey..."

"I know mom, it's fine."

After arriving at the front of the room, Chris shared short, quiet conversations with my family members, and they reluctantly offered their hands. You asshole, I thought.

After speaking briefly with my mother, he slinked over to me, head down. My teammates stood off to the side, watching it all.

"I have nothing to say to you, man," I said. He nodded. He paused for a moment, looking over at Mike. Then he faced me, and took off his glasses. His eyes were swollen and red from tears, and his quivering lips curled into his mouth.

He reached into his coat pocket, shaking, and handed me a small piece of folded, white paper. As soon as my fingers closed on it, he raced out the door, past my teammates, without even a pause to take a closer look at Mike. I looked down at the paper, playing with its edges and feeling the weight of the dozens of eyes that were locked on me. My mother made a move toward me, but I turned and walked toward the casket. There, over my brother's corpse, I unfolded the note, which said:

"Friendships are born on the field of athletic strife...Awards become corroded, friends gather no dust." - Jesse Owen

Just read this the other day – I'm SO sorry. Please tell your family too.

I leaned all my weight on the casket. Tremors raged through my legs and arms, and streams flowed from my nose and the corners of both eyes. I felt an arm wrap around my shoulders. Then a hand landed softly on my back. Then another. Soon all of my fighting brothers surrounded me and Mike, and together our quiet tears became a dirge. After a few sacred moments, I folded up the note again and placed it in the casket.

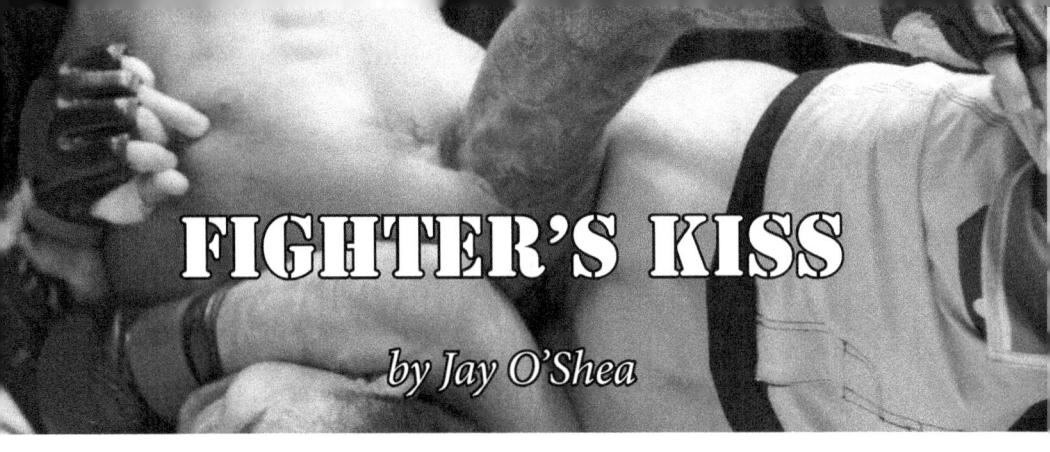

FIGHTER'S KISS

by Jay O'Shea

I end up sparring with the girl. It's her first day and she comes late. One of my students brings her. He's a tall guy, light skin and hair, a name so generic – Joe or John or Jim – I always forget it. He drives a shaky, old van and talks enough about his punk band that I've stopped asking. They come through the gate. From how they speak to each other, I know they're not a couple.

We're outside, training on cement, under the overhang. The mist burns off and the Southern California sun, even in March, is searing hot. This is all I have: a patch of grass and concrete behind a duplex in the San Gabriel Valley, neighbors who offer me the yard on Saturday mornings and weeknights. On Sundays, they barbecue where I train.

My students are all big white men, thick arms and thick middles. Teaching elephants to dance, my sifu said about training guys like this. The girl is small, with a brightness to her my boys have long since lost, if they ever had it. She stands apart from the others. But she doesn't clutch her arms around her chest or shift her weight as girls so often do.

Every once in a while, a woman comes to my class. They show up because they're afraid and want to be more confident. Or they want a workout. This isn't the art for that. We throw punches and sometimes we connect. We kick. We take each other down. Sometimes people get hurt. Nothing I can do about that.

The guys are thinking she's another one of those girls. I know better. I trained in Hong Kong and learned some stick fighting in the Philippines. When you get serious about the art, you train with girls, especially in Asia. There's so few of them, the good ones shine like gemstones. Some guys resent it; they say the girls have it easy. They're wrong. This is a man's world and the girls have courage stepping into class, let alone into the ring.

I stand off across from her. Our forearms touch. Bone and muscle press back at me. The charge of combat, even in play, comes off a body like electricity from a fallen wire.

She moves at me, a lot of power in that small frame. Hands heavy and fast. She gets through. I rock back. We crash in, hit and block as one. Our arms touch and I trap her hands. I come in with an elbow strike and stop at her shoulder. We connect again. I move in with a straight punch. She blocks and pushes back at my centerline. Our eyes meet. Hers are a rich color, brown with green undertones that catch the sunlight.

The force she throws around tells me she's used to sparring with guys bigger than me. Like them, she's easily tricked. I get her in an arm lock. She sees it, just before it happens. She's smiling as she rolls to the floor.

"Nice," she says, as if she's teaching me. I'm sweating as I reach out to help her up.

That's when I feel the glint, the one that comes when someone connects with this. A flicker, a match lighting in my chest: I can teach her.

"Who'd you learn Wing Chun from?" I ask, because she knows how to touch hands.

She tells me and we spend a few minutes trading names. The guys are watching. Her cheeks redden. But she smiles and doesn't look away.

"Learn to read the energy," I say toward the end of the class. "Look for what the other guy's telegraphing. Because unless he's really good, he's going to telegraph something."

When we shake hands, I step in and strike her shoulder. She grips my hand hard.

I set up my Wing Chun dummy in the yard. I tell myself it's a coincidence: a girl shows up who learned some Wing Chun as my interest in it revives. Maybe she sparked that interest. So what if she did? I didn't set up the dummy for her. I just wanted to start training with it again. Get the guys working their angles. It's good, focusing on that part of the system, the classical part.

She shows up on a Tuesday evening. Only the serious students come during the week. The sun's setting, casting my little yard in orange. The air takes on the cool tinge that comes when the sea breeze works its way across the LA basin, through downtown, and out here to the SGV. The girl walks up to the dummy. She slams her forearms against its arms, loops her hands around them and presses down, hitting its center with a palm strike. She's remembering one of the forms; I can see it come back to her.

She turns toward me.

"Oh." She stops. "Is it alright if I…?"

I shrug.

She's sparring with everyone now. They got used to her quicker than I expected. I tell a story about two girls I trained with in Hong Kong. Rough peasants from the desert. Strong as anyone. They fought each other in competition.

"Where do I find a girl like that?" One of the guys says.

"Hauling water in Mongolia," the girl says and they laugh.

I invite them in to watch UFC after we train. It's pretty informal around here. I couldn't do it any other way. Guys running laps around my yard and calling me sir: I'd feel like impostor. I don't even organize things like my teacher, with separate classes for different levels, training programs, any of that. The guys just hand me a folded-up check once a month.

My sifu never tried to keep me in his shadow; it just worked out that way. He's a great master. I'm a guy who worked hard and fought well. It's like that for everyone I know. The age of the great masters is over, I think.

But, still, when I bring the guys inside, it's awkward. I'm their sifu and I've got dishes in the sink and newspapers in the hallway. My Eskrima sticks stand off kilter, nunchaku coiled around them like a snake. My bookshelf is too small for my books and magazines and I haven't gotten around to getting a new one. I haven't gotten around to anything except keeping this school going. And training, of course.

The girl throws a black sweatshirt on over her tank top. Her sweatpants are black, too, and her nails are painted dark green. I feel an odd pang as I think about her in some club in Echo Park, making offhand mention of her Kung Fu class out in the middle of nowhere. I bet those rocker boys are impressed: who doesn't like a girl who kicks ass?

I offer her a beer and she holds up her hands, expecting me to toss it. I hand it to her instead. I wonder: does she ever let up? Is she girl outside and boy underneath?

Does it make a difference?

We sit on the couch, the guys on the floor, backs against the couch. They're deferring to us: the sifu and the girl. For once she doesn't object to being treated differently. Our arms touch and I feel wiry muscle and the edge of bone. Like touching hands outside. But now there's warmth between us.

UFC comes on, loud and bright. The Gracies file in, a dozen of them, a train of fathers, cousins, and brothers. Royce is up for a comeback fight. He stands off against some lug of a Greco-Roman wrestler, another dancing elephant. When the wrestler goes to shake his hand, Royce kisses him, once on each cheek. You'd think these guys would be used to Gracie kisses. But they're not and it's like the kiss is his first move.

I can barely keep my eyes on the screen.

She taps her bottle against mine. We look at each other as we drink. I catch the scent of musty sweat and something else running through it, sweet and organic.

The guys cheer. Gracie's got the wrestler down on his knees, in an arm lock. But the wrestler won't tap out. The girl looks at the TV.

"Awesome," she says.

She turns back to me. Sees I'm still watching her. But the moment has collapsed, crumpled under Royce's joint lock. She blushes. But it's not her warm, happy blush.

90

The UFC match gets me thinking about joint locking. I figure, enough of the Wing Chun, I'll focus on Jiu-Jitsu for a while. Next class, I demo a joint lock on the girl. She drops to her knees but, like Gracie's opponent, she won't tap out. I don't know what to do. I hit a couple of pressure points, to see if she'll react. Finally, she taps.

"My hand is numb," she laughs.

"You can take pain," I say. "Usually women… they… you know, they don't take pain so well."

"Yeah," she says as she stands up. "You try having a baby, Sifu."

I hadn't even thought about that. No one wears rings to class; we spar open hand and hit targets. There could be a husband. A boyfriend. Or just her and a kid.

She's smiling. But she's studying my expression, reading the energy, like I always say to. Her smile fades and I see it: I telegraphed and she stepped in with a Gracie kiss.

We stand off, connecting at the forearms. She comes straight at me: force toward my centerline, trying to break through. I block and her hand sweeps around, gliding over my arm as she tries to trap me. Then we're moving fast. Heavy. One punch after the next comes out of the web of our hands. She grabs my wrist, bars my other arm. I turn out of it, swinging around with a back fist as she steps in with a straight punch. I see it happen in slow motion. She doesn't have the control yet. I should have blocked.

At the last moment, she realizes. Pulls her punch. It makes contact anyway. My lower lip splits. A dry line of pain, then a trickle of blood.

She stares, not sure what to do. Her eyes lock onto mine. They flick to my bleeding lip.

I crack a smile. More blood.

"Control it," I say, because I'm supposed to.

She steps toward me and touches my lip. It stings but I don't pull away. She looks at the blood on her fingertip, then runs it along her mouth. Her tongue flicks out, my blood on her lip. An offering. A fighter's kiss.

GYM IN BLACK
BLACK HOUSE AND
THE ETHICAL MANAGER

by Michael Strayer

It sits adjacent to a busy street lined with warehouses and telephone poles; concrete; gray; lackluster in the smog-laced sunlight of Gardena, California. Looking at it, you would never think this the training grounds for some of the most savage fighters on the planet. Iron bars cross the lone window and you cannot see beyond the tinted glass. Only a black and white decal (a griffin, holding a grenade, lightning spewing from its mouth, wings outstretched and regal) stamped across the front door gives any indication of what this place is. Beneath the creature's feet in bold are the words:

BLACK HOUSE.

I pushed open the door, stepped inside, and stood, letting my eyes adjust. I was in a reception area, the floors carpeted, the air tinged with the smells of paint and dust. Ahead there was an empty room, a floor of raw concrete, stacks of cleaning supplies and tools heaped against the walls (the gym was undergoing remodels), and, further, the gym itself: a large dark cage, black matted floors, the far wall covered by a mural of Barack Obama (you know the one; originally by cult artist Shepard Fairey, with Obama gazing at something over the horizon, his eyes wistful and determined, the word HOPE across his chest). In this rendition, however, all spray-painted grays and blacks, his right eye is puffy and bruised, and beside him in black is a stencil of the White House, two words on either side:

Black House.

Originally established in Brazil as a training center for elite martial artists, the roster of fighters who call Black House home reads like a who's who list of MMA—Lyoto Machida, Glover Texiera, Cat Zingano, the Nogueira brothers, Anderson Silva (among many others). Founded and captained by Ed Soares and Jorge Guimares, the gym has become synonymous with success, a place where great warriors come together and hone their skills.

I was scheduled to interview Ed that afternoon. I sat on the couch in the waiting room—gold-colored and patterned with flamboyant, swirling flowers, elegant and absurd—and took in my surroundings. Hanging from every wall was framed fightwear. I gazed at a large white gi with a black belt, sweat-stained, embroidered with various logos. At the bottom was a gold plaque:

The gi Anderson Silva walked out in at UFC 117 against Chael Sonnen

August 7th, 2010

My gaze shifted along the walls. Every name I saw etched atop those tiny gold plaques sent a shiver of awe creeping through me. All belonged to champions, men who'd swum the "deep waters," as Sam Sheridan would say; men who'd bled and trained and fought and won before the screaming hordes of countless arenas across the globe. Men who trained here. In the wintry silence of the day the gym had a rarefied air, and the bits of used cloth and spandex pulsed with ineffable power... Like a temple of sorts, where parishioners of a different breed came to worship.

Ed Soares arrived following lunch with a fighter named Kevin Casey. He strode through the door, Casey in tow, an animated smile breaking his wide tan face. Entrepreneur-turned-fight manager, Ed Soares smiles often (and sincerely). Of Brazilian descent, he is heavyset and bald, with a hazy goatee and eyes like splashes of brown paint. He carries himself with confidence, and immediately makes you feel like you're one of his friends.

He directed me to his office. This room, in contrast to the gym, was radiant and clean—the furniture white, the walls decorated in graffiti-coated canvases of famous black men (Don King, Tupac, Biggie Smalls), a portrait of Bruce Lee, a massive and vibrantly decorated 'E,' all in the style of street art.

I asked him about the paintings.

"I love it," he said, his face brightening. "Bruce Lee is done by this graffiti artist named Donkey Boy, who did Obama in the

Black House gym… These are all done by a local artist in my neighborhood named Steve Frankle (A.K.A 'Stein')… I've been collecting his art for many, many years." He gestured at the picture of King. "These are just a few pieces that I have… Actually…" He rose suddenly from his chair and came around the desk. "The newest piece that I got from him is this one right here."

He stooped. When he straightened he was holding another image of Bruce Lee, a painting of the actor as he looked in the climactic scene of Enter the Dragon. Ed held the piece at arms' length and observed it proudly. "That's 1992," he said. He speaks faster as he gets excited. "One of my best friends had it and I've wanted it for so many years and on my birthday, a couple weeks ago, he gave it to me."

He returned to his seat and pointed at the E. "And this one right here was made by a famous graffiti artist from Los Angeles… named Risk… I'm not an artist, but I love graffiti art."

He attributes this love to his childhood in L.A., a city awash in a scintillating smudge of spray-paint, as well as his time as a club promoter and manger of hip hop bands. Alongside urban art, his other passion, mixed martial arts, also has its roots in his southern Californian upbringing—Gracie Jiu-jitsu.

"You know my parents are Brazilian, and I grew up here in Redondo Beach, California, in the South Bay… And I trained jiu-jitsu. I started training with Royce [Gracie], and I've been friends with Royce for a long time. I never looked to fighting as a career, I was always just a big fan, and there was a time I owned my own clothing line—which was Sinister Brand Clothing—and, as a fan of mixed martial arts, I would sponsor these guys, back when nobody sponsored them."

His initial fame in the fight business came with Chuck Liddell's notorious icicle shorts, which Ed designed. From there, he began creating customized, signature clothing for fighters to wear as they walked towards the cage.

"The first fighter brand tee-shirt was a Sinister Chuck Liddell tee-shirt. Before that there were no fighters with signature tees. With that said, we went to Japan in 2003 when Chuck fought Quinton [Jackson] in the Pride Grand Prix. At that time I ran into my now current business partner, Jorge. He did a t.v. show in Brazil called 'Passing the Guard.' And I was hanging out with him, and he was like 'Hey man I need a cameraman for my show this week... You wanna be my cameraman?' So I was like, 'Sure.' And all week long I was shooting everything."

This chance meeting proved pivotal in both men's lives. Ed offered to conduct the post-fight interviews in U.S.-based shows for Jorge's program, thinking that—at first—it would provide great exposure for his clothing line.

"And you know I flew home from Japan, and that was in November of 2003, and I thought: I don't just wanna do interviews. I wanna bring this show to the U.S."

He closed a deal with KDOC—a local network that covers all of L.A. County, Orange County, and parts of Ventura and San Diego Counties. By the end of the first season, they were the second highest-rated show Saturday nights and midnight in their region. At that point, Dana White—the president of the UFC—started buying advertising on their program, and the rest, in Ed's words, is history.

"I built a good relationship with all the fight organizations and fighters, my business partner being kinda like a Larry Merchant of Brazil when it comes to MMA. And we started saying, 'Hey... Why don't we just bring fighters from Brazil to fight in the UFC?'"

He smiled. "And here we are."

Today, as the manager of several premiere fighters in mixed martial arts (including former UFC middleweight champion Anderson Silva, as well as former light-heavyweight champion Lyoto Machida), he is considered one of the more influential people in the sport. When asked about the reason behind his success, why so many top athletes seek him out, he is humble and demurs slightly.

"You know what," he said. "I don't know what it is... That would be a question for them. When I got into this sport, one of my goals was to prove you could be a successful manager, and be ethical, and do the right thing. That was first and foremost. I had a successful clothing company. I didn't get into managing for the money; I got into it because it was something I wanted to do. I wanted to prove that you can do both: You can do the right thing and still be successful. And I think I'm proof of that.

"Nowadays people see the relationship that we have with the UFC and what we've been able to do with some of our fighters. Fortunately, we made the right picks in the beginning; we picked the right guys to go with. It's a combination of opportunity and luck and it all met up at the same place. And that's success."

According to Ed, there are no typical days in the life of a fight manager. "For instance today," he told me. "This morning I wake up at 8:15 and five minutes later get a text from Anderson: 'Hey bro can we meet up?'

"So today I woke up and went to breakfast with Anderson and we had a great talk.... I ran some errands, came here, went out to lunch with Kevin Casey, and now I'm doing an interview... Every day's a little different. It's a lot of moving parts. Whether it's making sure guys' fights are right, or they're getting the right endorsement deals... You name it... It's like, 'Thank God I'm doing what I love.'"

When Ed speaks of his fighters, he does so nonchalantly, and you almost forget that when he mentions "going to breakfast with Anderson," he's referring to Anderson Silva, regarded by many as the greatest mixed martial artist to ever compete. Silva boasts the longest undefeated reign in UFC history, a streak spanning 2457 days and 10 consecutive title defenses, and which ended violently on July 6th, 2013, to current middleweight champion, Chris Weidman.

Says Ed, on Silva:

"He's one of the special ones. I have no doubt in my mind. People say I'm biased because he's my client, but I'm telling you: to me it's like watching Michael Jordan play basketball, or Muhammad Ali box, or Tiger Woods golf. I think he's one of the greatest of all times, and he'll go down as the greatest of all times, and in any great of combat sport you always see a guy who's been a champion have a stumble in his career, and I think his fight with Chris Weidman was that. We actually talked about that this morning. And it was funny, because when we talked, he was like 'I just woke up and it wasn't my day. I didn't feel right, I didn't feel good.'

"That's very unlike him… He just said, 'Ed it wasn't my day.' But people can say what they want, one thing is he takes his training very serious, and he's dedicated, and he's just one of those guys—he had that gift, and that was the gift God gave him, and he's embraced it." He clasped his hands together. "And look what he's been able to create."

The night of Silva's loss is seared into Ed's memories, and, when questioned about it, he grows quiet and very still.

"It just sucks to see someone…" he said, at length. "He's not just a client. To see someone you care about knocked out on the mat… It's not easy to see. That's what went through my mind. And then I can say I was in a little bit of shock, almost, like disbelief. I didn't believe it happened.

"When I saw him drop, I didn't see that shot hit him, I just saw him drop… And then, boom, he got hit one more time and the ref stopped the fight."

As of this writing, the rematch between Silva and Weidman is set for December 28, 2013. I asked Ed what will make the second fight different.

"I think Anderson's hungry again," he said. "You go seven years of your life being the greatest fighter of all time, and people tell you how great you are, eventually that's gonna effect you. I don't care how humble or down to earth you are… Sometimes it gets away from you. He goes from living a very humble life and not really having a car to having anything he wants… From not owning a house to having houses in different countries. Anderson's a good guy, a good-hearted guy, but sometimes with all that pressure it just gets to you."

Ed describes his connection to his star client as brotherly ("He's part of my family," he says), with the ups and downs that come with such close association. He loves Silva, and is unerringly honest in his rapport with the fighter, which can—at times—lead to discomfort and anger. "At the end of the day I'm his friend, and I want what's best for him, and I tell him what I think all the time. I don't tell him what he wants to hear… Whether it's right or wrong, I tell him what I believe."

"What did you tell him after the Weidman fight?" I asked.

He looked at me, brow raised. "I didn't tell him much. A few days after he said that he didn't wanna fight, he didn't wanna rematch and all that... It was weird. I walked into his gym and we looked at each other... And I said, 'Hey, we gotta do this rematch.'

"And he said: 'We'll have that belt back before the end of the year.'"

We continued to talk about Ed's life as a manager. While some in his profession choose a more participatory role in their fighters' training, Ed maintains his distance. "I really don't get involved too much in their training," he said. "I'm there for them if they need help...I feel that they're professionals, and I'm not gonna tell them what they need to do to win the fight, the same way they're not gonna tell me how to negotiate a contract."

We spoke of the Resurrection Fighting Alliance (RFA), of which Ed is the president. "We're kinda like the farm league for the UFC. When I came into the RFA the first thing I said was, 'I wanna be the developmental league for the UFC.' And the first thing I did was get a t.v. deal, and then I closed a deal with the UFC to be the only other organization that has the license to use an Octagon." He likens the affiliation between the RFA and the UFC to that of college football and the NFL, and many of the top contenders in the sport have emerged from the promotion.

"These new kids are animals," he said. "They're young, they're hungry, and they're highly skilled mixed martial artists."

Having accomplished so much, I wondered about the kind of legacy Ed hoped to leave behind in the fight world.

He said, "I just think about... when I die, I guess... I just want people to remember that I'm a good guy. I think that's the biggest compliment I could get. I'm no angel, I've made my mistakes, but at the end of the day I always try to do the right thing...

"One moment that sticks out in my mind is when I took José Aldo to his first NBA game. We sat courtside, and after that night I remember going back to the hotel and he looked at me and he said,

'That was one of the greatest nights of my life.'

"It had nothing to do with fighting, but it was something that because of fighting I was able to do. I like helping people… And being a part of someone's life to achieve what they set out to do… if I can contribute to that and help them get where they wanna go… That's what life's about."

In the end, Ed Soares is a fight fan, doing what he loves, and he attributes this passion to his success. "I'm truly doing what I love… And if you do something you love, you'll never work another day in your life. Now: I feel like I work my ass off. But I love what I do, man."

We stood. Ed led me down the silent halls of the gym. Kevin Casey was just finishing a photo-shoot, and we paused to speak with him, the spray-painted visage of Barack Obama squinting down at us from the wall above the cage.

Later, driving home, I passed a graffiti-tagged billboard advertising the Silva/Weidman rematch and grinned.

TWO WEEKS, ONE NIGHT IN SACRAMENTO

by Brian Jungwiwattanaporn

"Last round!" said Mike as the timer sounded. Lee punched his gloves together, their snug reassurance offsetting the look of exhaustion on his face. Raising his hands to his chin he thought about spitting out his mouth guard. Lee felt he could dance around for three more minutes if only he could breathe. Roger moved from across the ring, smiling, bouncing on his toes. Two weeks from fight time and he was reaching his peak. Lee pawed his jab, knowing it was slow. Roger slipped his head and moved forward, changing his level. Crouching low, he drove a hook into Lee's body. The next three minutes felt long.

"Time!" Mike said as a buzz sounded from the corner. Lee lay on the canvas looking at the ceiling. Turning his head he spat out his mouth guard and clutched his side. He remembered the final punch and sinking to the floor. Roger stood over him, face enclosed in headgear with his glove extended. Lee raised his hand to bump fists, "Good job," said Roger before ducking under the ropes and moving to the wrestling mats.

Lee watched the rest of practice, wrestling takedowns and then cardio. Roger still had to drop five pounds before fight night. "He's coming along pretty well," said Lee.

Mike nodded, "Still needs to work on his clinch game, but he's got a nice sprawl now. How's your rib?"

"It's okay, just winded."

"Are you coming by tomorrow? We need another body in the rotation. The only way to push Roger is to keep feeding him fresh guys."

Lee grinned, "Yeah sure."

Driving home, Lee looked forward to ice and ibuprofen.

101

Stretching after class he noticed all of the little aches that were overshadowed by being punched and kicked in the head and body. He allowed himself a smile, a grudging self-respect even if the session played with his confidence. It was a painful privilege to train with professional fighters. Lee remembered his first day at the gym last year, just dropping by to watch after another lonely ten-hour work day. The men were merciless, beating on each other, slamming their bodies against the mat. He'd almost left, but wanted to at least talk to the trainer, show he was interested. By the time he finished meeting Mike, the atmosphere had changed, the people around the gym sat and stretched, they laughed and smiled before getting ready to go to dinner together. A family in a city full of strangers. Lee couldn't remember the last time he went to happy hour with his co-workers, but he desperately wanted to hang out with this group of guys.

Lee signed up, and Mike asked him his goals. Weight loss, competition, confidence, self-defense, Lee agreed to all of them though he could never articulate what he really wanted. Lee didn't just want to test himself, he wanted the pain and suffering a true test required. Something that was missing from his office cubicle. He wanted to know if he was brave, if he had courage, but he could never say it. Bravery was what children talked about, it felt silly to discuss, but Lee knew it was the key he was missing. The reason he stayed behind his desk, the reason he couldn't ask a girl on a date, the reason why he needed to be here, to know if he measured up to the idea he wanted to be.

Undoing the straps of the kicking pads, Lee looked at his forearms dappled by dark purple bruises. Roger's Muay Thai session was thankfully over, kicks and knees buried themselves into the pads that Lee held. Roger bit the velcro strap on his glove and pulled, loosening the glove, "Jits?" he said.

Lee nodded, he loved Brazilian Jiu-Jitsu even if the gi caused abrasions across his face. He was able to grip the uniform and slow some of the stronger fighters down, eventually using his leverage to set up sweeps and submissions. Mike intervened, "No time for BJJ today, I want MMA sparring instead. Full go. Stand up, takedowns, and groundwork. Five minute rounds."

"Sure thing," said Roger, already strapping the smaller MMA gloves to his hands. He was bouncing, keeping his heart rate up. Lee took a swig of water. Too tired to speak, he raised his thumbs. He watched Roger for the first two rounds before he cycled in as the fresh opponent. Lee always played "what if," when he watched other fighters move around the gym. What if he had never become an accountant, what if he quit his job and moved to Brazil or Thailand for a year, what if he was ten or fifteen years younger? Lee took his turn, jumping on Roger immediately, and his questions melted away.

"Good work," said Mike, "You coming in tomorrow?"

Lee sat unwrapping sports tape from his fingers, a minor hurt on his list of injuries. "Gotta work. Day job stuff."

"Yeah, no worries," Mike said, "Try to make it if you can though, it's a team sport and we need you here too."

Lee nodded and took a shower, he never liked the clinging scent of his sweat mingled with a half dozen other men. He thought of Mike's favorite refrain, MMA was a team sport, and appreciated the notion. Roger would be in the cage alone with another man trying to knock him out or beat him down, but everyone in the gym helped him to prepare. They were his biggest fans, and they each claimed a small piece of Roger's success for themselves.

Clicking through internet forums, Lee settled on watching a stream of instructional videos. He wanted something new to bring, some flashy Jiu-Jitsu to surprise everyone at the gym, and maybe give Roger a challenge. Work was a bore in comparison, and he'd already missed a week of class. Lee tried to maintain his discipline, Mike had him jogging on the days he couldn't make it to the gym, and he focused on the holy trinity of pushups, sit ups, and squats when he was at home. Lee glanced at the clock, accounts could wait for tomorrow, he left his computer and made his way to practice.

"Oh man, Roger, I'm sorry," said Lee once he arrived, "What happened?"

"Torn ACL," said Roger resting in a chair, his knee was bandaged, and a pair of crutches lay against his shoulder.

"Heel hook?"

"No, just flubbed a take down," said Roger, "It happens."

Lee sat down on the mat, "So what now?" he said knowing the answer. It wasn't the first knee destroyed in training.

"I had the surgery over the weekend. I'm out for the rest of the year."

"It's been a busy week since you've been gone," said Mike walking towards them. "You feeling okay, Roger?" "Yeah, just wanted to watch the guys." "And you Lee, feel like working out?"

"Yeah, I wanted to help Roger get ready, but I can work in with the other guys." Mike looked at Roger who shrugged and said "Why not?"

"How would you like to fight on Saturday?" said Mike, "Roger's opponent is free and he's your weight. The promoter needs someone and he's relying on our gym."

"Um, what?" said Lee, "Seriously?"

Mike said, "He's two-and-one. His boxing is decent, but his takedown defense is horrible."

"You've been training with the fight team for four months, and you've helped me get ready for my last fight," said Roger. "I think you're ready."

Lee raised his palms. "I'm thirty-six years old," he said, "and an accountant."

"This kid is younger, but your style matches up well. I think you can take him," said Mike.

Lee looked at his friends again. They had hurt each other, bled and bruised with one another on a near weekly basis. Lee exhaled and ran his fingers through his receding hair, "Sure, screw it, why not?"

Fight night arrived sooner than Lee had hoped. The last week was mostly light drilling and pep talks from Mike and Roger. Lee was lucky that he didn't have to cut any weight, but it probably wouldn't have been a problem since he ended up vomiting when they arrived at the venue. Mike said it was nerves, and Roger reassured him that the same thing happened to him his first time as well. Lee slipped into a pair of gray board shorts and Mike wrapped his hands.

"You're carrying the gym's flag tonight," Mike said guiding Lee's fingers into a glove, "Don't worry, you've sparred with guys twice as scary as this kid. You know everything to do, you've seen every position. Just remember, stay relaxed. Breathe, move, and then try to hit him. Make us proud."

"You got this," said Roger handing over a mouth guard.

Looking back, Lee couldn't remember the first two rounds. There was the bell and then the adrenaline took over. He took a few knees to the stomach and maybe a punch or two, but was so amped he didn't feel a thing. His vision was narrow and his ears shut down. He couldn't hear the crowd cheering, only an occasional screamed instruction from Mike or Roger. Mostly only heard his own heavy breathing. He barely noticed when the referee cut between him and his opponent and signaled them to their corners.

Lee leaned against the cage as Mike slid a stool under his legs and then knelt in front of him. "You're doing good. I need you to breathe now. Remember practice? This is just like the gym."

Focusing his vision, Lee's brain snapped to attention, he wanted to say, "This is crazy! That kid is trying to kill me," but instead he just nodded. He could hear the crowd now, and he had to blink the brightness of the arena's lights out of his eyes. He missed the rest of what Mike was trying to say, catching only the end as the stool was pulled from under him and he was forced to stand up.

"I want circle-jab, circle-jab, and then a two-three-two when he lets down his guard," said Mike, rushing to get out of the cage.

Lee circled, his jab snapped out and he circled away from the counter. Two-three-two, a cross, hook, and then another cross. He missed the first two punches but felt the solid, satisfying thud of his hand connecting on the third. Rushing forward, Lee dove for a double-leg takedown. He felt the burn in his legs as he kept driving ahead, it was all he could remember to do, keep moving, keep going forward. He took his opponent to the ground. Lee climbed up his opponent's body eagerly, and then found himself on his back. He'd been swept. All of the air went from lungs as the younger man settled his weight upon Lee's chest. Lee turned his head and saw the clock, four and half minutes to go.

Lee tried to move, but his body refused. Too tired and too much weight resting on his hips. Lee felt small slaps on his head and body. He could hear the crowd cheering now, though he was unsure if they were encouraging him or wanting to see him brutalized. "Screw it." he thought as he dug his heels into the floor. He pushed his opponent's hips away and created enough space to wrap his legs around his abuser. Lee felt relief, he managed the guard position, his favorite. A punch landed on his nose and he felt his eyes beginning to tear up, no time to celebrate the small successes. The man raised his fist again, and Lee pushed his leg up, resting it on the man's shoulder. He pulled his opponent's head forward and started working a triangle choke. Lee didn't think he could finish the submission, it was loose, his legs were jelly, and his opponent was slippery. Small punches peppered his ribs, Lee punched back. He yelled, vicious and life-affirming. He might lose, but he wouldn't be defeated.

Eventually, the bell rang. His opponent rolled off of him and Lee lay on the canvas. He spat out his mouth guard, and covered his face with his hands. The arena was yelling, clapping, and stomping their feet on the bleachers. Lee felt as if his chest was exploding, and he focused on getting his breath back. Tears started rolling from his eyes. He wasn't sure if it was from the hit to the nose, or the release of stress, and he didn't care. He stood and bumped fists with the younger man before embracing him. "Good one," he said.

Mike's shoulders pushed into Lee's knees and he was hoisted upwards. Lee saw Roger and reflected his friend's grin. "Sorry coach, I tried," Lee said. "What's the judge's decision?"

Letting his friend down, Mike smiled "What do you think? Does it even matter?"

It was infinitely amusing to laugh and cry at the same time. Lee raised his arms and cheered.

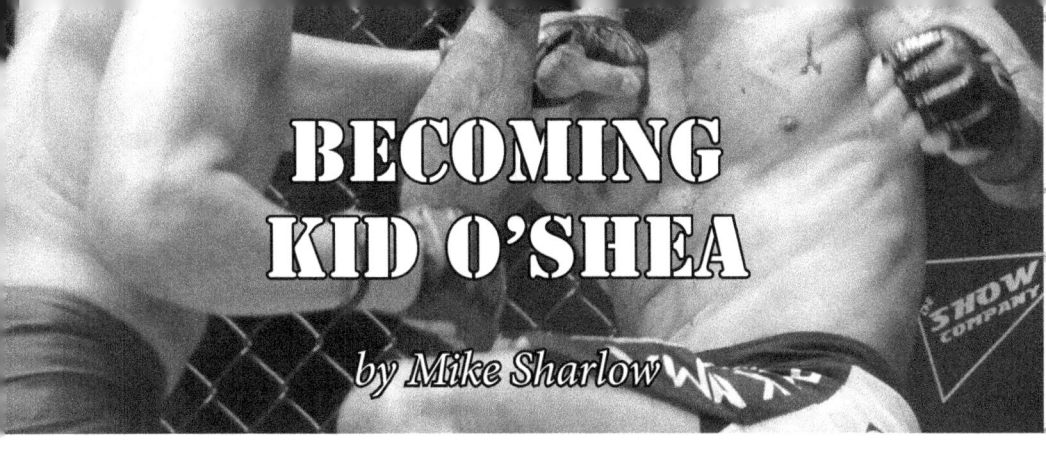

BECOMING KID O'SHEA

by Mike Sharlow

I worked out, whether it was weights at the Y, running, riding bike (a Trek 400), or many variations of pull ups and dips on the monkey bars in the park near my apartment. Lately the park was where I worked out. I was in pretty good shape. Actually, I was in the best shape of my life, and I was twenty-two. I was a little over five foot seven, and I weighed about one-thirty-five. I didn't work out to compete in anything. I worked out to look good, to be bigger. I liked the idea of being in shape, but it was primarily a pursuit in vanity.

Every other day I walked the three blocks to the park through the playground of the old grade school, Washburn. The school closed down quite a few years ago, but the school district rented out space to whomever. Part of the third floor was used by the local boxing club. I knew this because a friend's dad, who used to be a fighter, ran it. His name was George "Tiger" Markos. He fought in the mid- to late-1930s. Supposedly, he was once a contender.

Last November my friend George Jr. and I sat at a bar and watched the Ray "Boom Boom" Mancini fight Duk Koo Kim. It was a brutal toe-to-toe slugfest. Mancini stopped Kim in the 14th round. Minutes later Kim lost consciousness and slipped into a coma. Four days later he died. George Jr. told me while we watched the fight that his Dad ran a boxing club in Washburn, the old grade school. I told George Jr. that I would like to work out there. He told me that his Dad wouldn't mind. "Just show up," he said.

Months later I finally walked into the school. I was wearing my black high top Chuck Taylors, gray sweat pants, and a white t-shirt. I bought hand wraps about a week before at the sporting goods store downtown. I knew I would need something to protect my hands when hitting the heavy bag.

There was no sign to tell anyone where the boxing gym was,

107

but I knew from George Jr. that it was on the third floor. The wood stairs creaked and echoed loudly with each step I took. The city was thinking about razing this building. Shame to lose all of the beautiful woodwork and high ceilings.

Reaching the third floor I heard sounds of the gym. I walked in and saw two guys sparring in the ring. George Markos leaned over the curtain barking directions at the fighters. There were three heavy bags and two speed bags lined up by the window. There was a small locker room attached, and I went inside and sat on the bench to wrap my hands. I had been practicing this for days so I could do it expertly and quickly when I went to the gym.

The wood floor creaked loudly as I took the long walk over to one of the empty heavy bags. I watched one of the other fighters working the bag and I mimicked his action. He just sort of pounded away with thudding shots that echoed through the gym. In a couple of minutes George came over to me and asked me if I'd ever fought. He sort of mumbled, so I had to think about what he asked me. Then I said, "No, not really."

Then he said, "Lef, lef, rye. Lef, lef, rye. Do 'at"

I followed his direction and continually threw the combination.

"Fas' s'can," he said.

I did what he asked, but I also switched up my combinations, doing what felt right. I let my hands go without thinking about it.

"Good," he said.

Reverberating in my head and in the gym I heard, "Ba-dadada-dada" over and over, as I hit the bag until my arms ached, and I had to stop.

"Ver' good," he said. "C'mn ba' tomma."

"Okay." I looked around and noticed the other four fighters staring at me. I immediately thought there must be something wrong with me. It seemed like it was closing time, so I walked back to the locker room to remove my wraps. As I was rolling my wraps, the rest of the fighters came into the locker room. One sat right next to me.

"Nice hand speed, man," he said.

"Yeah thanks," I said.

"Comin' back tomorrow?" he asked.

"I think so."

"You should," he said and held out his hand to give him five.

I hit it firmly and informally without display.

"See ya."

My girlfriend was waiting back at the apartment.

"Where have you been?" she asked.

"Working out at the boxing gym."

"What boxing gym?"

"There's one at the old school."

"Since when?"

"Since—I don't know. I heard about it a couple of months ago." Then I told her everything, particularly that they asked me to come back. She listened attentively.

She was a beauty, but she hadn't always been. At twenty, about the time I met her, she blossomed. And since then I had been the beneficiary of her firm femininity and pretty face. She was a hundred and five pounds and four inches shorter than me. I knew by her posture, as she stood there in her bare feet that she wanted me to fuck her. I wasn't a proponent of the "no sex while training for a fight" rule.

I sat on the couch, and she straddled me. I pulled at her shorts and panties. She adjusted nimbly on my lap. As she rocked on top of me, I wondered what other women felt like inside. I knew that she knew other men before me. I knew that she was with other men while she was with me. Would she cry when I left her? Because I also knew, after my day at the gym, that someday I would leave her. It wasn't just that she was a cheater. If that was the case, I would have left her a long time ago.

I finally knew why I stayed with her. She had something other than me. She had a future that could exist without me. She was almost finished with her undergrad degree in chemistry and would soon be on her way to graduate school at the University of Wisconsin in Madison. I was a dropout wannabe writer—unpublished—who worked as a night janitor at a motel and restaurant. She had a lucrative future. My only chance at a lucrative future was with her. Call me a slug, a leech, or a loser, but there was nothing more sobering than knowing your own fate could be cleaning shit splattered restroom stalls and emptying cracker box tin bins filled with bloody sanitary napkins. She had always seemed like my only way out. Until today when I went to the gym, the only practical skill I had was screwing her to orgasm.

The next day I did some stretching at home and then I jogged the couple of blocks over to the school. I hadn't really worked up a sweat, but I was warm. I was afraid I was going to be too early, but all the guys that were there before were already at work, plus one more new guy. I wrapped my hands quickly and went into the gym.

If anyone noticed me, they didn't show it. Yesterday they urged me to come back and today they could care less. Fuck it, I thought, and I began hitting a speed bag, slowly at first to acquire any sort of rhythm since I wasn't sure how successful I would be. Years ago my Dad had brought home an old used speed bag and hung it in the garage. I got pretty good at it, but the last time I hit one I was teenager. It came back to me like riding a bike. The rhythm was hypnotic, and I went faster and faster until I could go no more and had to stop. I accentuated the end with one hard left. BA-DOW! It echoed throughout the gym. Then I noticed that everyone had been watching me, and now they were going back to their own work.

Mr. Markos walked over to me. "You spa'?"

"Spar? Haven't yet," I said. When I was a kid, my Dad bought my brothers and me two pair of sixteen ounce Rocky Graziano boxing gloves. They got a lot of use. We pounded on each other, the neighborhood kids, and our Dad. There wasn't anything formal about this training, but there was something to be said for punching and getting punched.

I followed Mr. Markos over to the ring and he handed me a pair of black Everlast gloves. I think they were fourteen ounces. They were well worn, but still completely intact. Mr. Markos helped me on with my gloves and tied them. He pulled the head gear on me and yanked the chin strap tight.

Mr. Markos yelled at one of the guys working out on a heavy bag. The guy knew what Mr. Markos wanted, because he grabbed a pair of gloves and head gear. One of the other fighters helped him on with his gloves and head gear. If that guy hit me as hard as he punched the heavy bag, I was in trouble.

Mr. Markos led me around to a rickety set of wood risers, so I could enter the ring. The fighter I was going to spar was already in the ring. Inside the ropes, the ring seemed smaller and my sparring partner looked bigger. He was about my height, maybe a little shorter, but he was stocky. He probably outweighed me by at least ten pounds. He had on gray sweat pants with black boxing trunks over them. When I first saw him hitting the heavy bag he was wearing a gray sweatshirt. He had taken it off, and now he was wearing a white tank top. He shuffled in his corner. He had real boxing shoes. He shadowboxed in his corner and champed his jaw violently. I wondered how his teeth could take it, but then I saw that he a mouth guard in. I turned towards Mr. Markos and pointed at my mouth and showed him my teeth. He put up his hand, mumbled something, and then walked off, bent over with short quick steps. His body looked a bit wrecked, but he moved gracefully and covered ground in a hurry. He awkwardly tore open a package with his gnarly fingers and rinsed it in the white school drinking fountain. When he got to the ring he told me to bend over the ropes, and he expertly slid the guard into my mouth. Not properly molded, but better than nothing. It was bitter and wet. Mr. Markos' hands were ugly and broken, but they looked clean.

A bell rang, one piercing note that made me jump. I looked down to see Mr. Markos holding the bell and looking back at me. Then he looked at my opponent, like I should be looking at him. I tentatively moved towards him, but he covered the ring and almost met me in my corner. He threw a hard jab and bounced it off my forehead. I was instantly pissed that he landed the punch. It stunned me a bit. I saw it coming but didn't move. I know I could have avoided it, and I proved it when he threw the next one.

I threw my own and doubled it up. He threw a left hook, and I backed away and slid to my left. His punch grazed my shoulder. I threw a left-right combination that landed solidly. I didn't throw it hard, so it didn't do much damage, but it did irritate him. He stepped up his pursuit and cut off the ring. I was surprised at how quick he could be. He trapped me against the ropes and pounded me. I covered up and most of the punches landed on my shoulders and gloves. I heard Mr. Markos yelling at me. I couldn't hear what he was saying, but I know he wanted me off the ropes. Then my opponent landed a solid shot on my head. I saw lightning flash, blue-white stars sparkling. I had felt this before. When I was a kid my Dad used to smack me on the head when he got pissed off. The shot usually came out of nowhere. Sometimes my Dad hit my brothers and I just because we were there, in striking distance. I knew it would pass quickly. I clinched my opponent, and before he pushed me off, I slid around him to the center of the ring. After my Dad used to hit me, I cried but always felt angry and wanted to strike back. In this case my reaction was the same, except I could actually hit back. I felt this burst of energy, a controlled explosion, and I let my hands go.

Wherever I wanted them to hit, they landed. It didn't even feel like I was thinking about what I wanted to do. I battered my opponent with a flurry. My barrage of punches put him on the defensive. When he covered his head, I ripped him to the body. When he pulled his elbows down, I whacked him in the head. The accumulation of punches backed him up, but I couldn't tell whether I was really hurting him, so after I tapped him on the head and he exposed his ribs a bit, I took one quick step to my left and dug a left to his body. I threw my whole body into that punch and it landed cleanly and solidly with a thud! He grunted and bent favoring his side, and I knew I hurt him. He exposed his head, and I threw a quick right to measure distance, and followed it up with a straight hard left to his chin. His eyes rolled, and he fell on his face. I heard Mr. Markos yelling. I stepped back, nearly to the other side of the ring. Mr. Markos climbed into the ring and went to my opponent's aide.

I climbed out of the ring, and another fighter came over to

help me with my gloves and head gear. "What's your name, man?" he asked.

"Mick," I said, "O'Shea." I was still breathing hard and my heart was pounding.

"Irish kid, huh?" He smiled.

"I guess. You?"

"Danny Thompson. Danny "Tommy Gun" Thompson. Heard of me?"

"Maybe," I said, but I hadn't.

Mr. Markos came over and grabbed the head gear and gloves. He looked pissed off.

"Kid took it to him, huh Mr. Markos?" Danny said. "A lightweight piss-pounding a middleweight, a decent middleweight."

A smile crept to the corner of Mr Markos' mouth. "G' job, Kid. Gonna make a fighter outta you. Ya make it look easy. Be here t'morrow 'gin."

"He thinks you got somethin'." Danny thought for a second, and then said, "You do got somethin'. I ain't seen hand speed like that in a long time. Can hit, too. Mr. Markos is right. Ya do make it look easy. "

"I'm looking for a place to live. Know of anywhere?" I asked.

"Me and a couple of the guys from here live together. We have an empty bedroom. Been lookin' for another roommate. A hundred a month. You in?" he asked.

"Yeah, I'm definitely in," I said.

BANG MUAY THAI AND THE WINGED WARRIOR

by Michael Strayer

The entrance to Elite MMA is situated at the foot of a stairwell, the gym being mostly underground, and small, almost hidden. Descending those steps you feel as if entering a new world and, stepping inside, you're immediately aware of the smells of rubber, disinfectant, and sweat. Then you hear it—the sound. Grunting, and gasps for air. You hear music, and voices, men and women spurring each other on, and the bright rattle of chains—heavy-bags swaying— and the soft mute whumping of fists and leather.

The first thing you see, as you walk past the front desk, is a cage—black, impersonal—and beyond the lightless rungs a television, playing fights. Everywhere you look you're reminded that you're in a place for fighters—in the gloves dangling from the walls and the championship belts above them—in the bouncing bags and training tools and the crash of iron plates—in the sweating, red-faced people moving about, legs bruised, ears gnarled and misshapen.

In a large room in the back of the gym a group of thirty or so has gathered. They are there for a Muay Thai seminar, and they stand before the mirrored wall, shadowboxing. They wear ankle wraps and glossy shorts in the style of Thai boxers, their heads shaved or hair tied back, tattooed, determined, focused, beginning to sweat. Already the morning is hot. It is late August, 2013, and warmth pulses from the valley in which Elite MMA is located—Thousand Oaks, California— and hot light streams into the room from a high-window.

Between the light, between the fighters, he moves, scrutinizing every detail. Even now, in the warm-up, he analyzes the trainees' movements—searching for mistakes, bad habits, glitches to correct. His eyes miss nothing. He too wears Thai shorts, his of a vibrant orange, and a white tee shirt. On its back is an image of a winged warrior, also in shorts, wings outspread, arms wide and knee raised, as if alighting *into some celestial battle. Beneath this is a single word:*

"Bang."

He instructs the fighters to put on their gloves and break into pairs. He calls out combinations—Jab/Hook, Hook/Cross—and watches as they practice, using each other's hands as targets, eagle-eyed.

"Remember," he reminds them…

"You can have their hands in your face, or your hands in their face. The choice is yours." Duane "Bang" Ludwig gestured for his assistant, UFC bantamweight T.J. Dillashaw, to help him demonstrate. They squared off, fists clenched. "Two punches, two steps," he said, stepping forward and punching simultaneously. "Don't move, then punch… Blend the two together. Simple, no?"

A former UFC fighter, Muay Thai world champion, and current head coach of Team Alpha Male, Ludwig's strikes slashed the air with a practiced efficiency. The seminar resumed. The noise of gloves smacking gloves, the thunderous popping of leather on leather—*Cross, Hook! Cross, Hook!*—ricocheted across the mats. Hair darkened; sweat sprouted from foreheads. Explosions of breath sounded in time with the punches—*Chh-shh! Chh-shh! Chh-shh!*

Ludwig walked amongst the students, correcting posture, answering questions. His explanations were simple and methodic. His smile never left. His eyes glinted with enthusiasm as he observed his flock of fighters, drilling on the mats.

"I love coaching," he says. "I love living through these fighters and these athletes."

Ludwig, who holds the UFC record for the fastest knockout (6.06 seconds against Jonathan Goulet), was once regarded as one of the most feared strikers in the sport. But a three-fight losing streak culminating in a torn knee-ligament culled his meteoric potential, cutting short his career, and causing him to re-evaluate his chosen path. For him, the decision to coach was simple, and he's since found true happiness at Team Alpha Male—based out of Sacramento— teaching, traveling, and hosting seminars ("Seminars," writes Sam Sheridan in *A Fighter's Heart*, "are a big part of the martial arts business… They are a way for professional martial artists to support themselves… Seminars offer a valuable opportunity to see and learn from great fighters." And Ludwig, having quit competition, still needed to provide for his family, as well as satiate his passion for fighting.)

His attitude regarding these circumstances is one of thankfulness.

"I'm a much happier human being now," he says, "than I ever was as a fighter."

The seminar unfolded and the drills became more complex. "Before, during, and after," he yelled. "Something is happening. Look for those clues. There's always an opening."

The students moved, back and forth, attacking and defending. In one corner of the room, watching, Ludwig's wife, Jessica, and their two children sat. Her eyes glistened as her husband lectured; a serene smile stretched atop her face, and now and again Ludwig would break away from class to come and kiss her on the head, or hug his daughter, or pick up his son.

"I've known Duane for so many years," said Jessica, as her husband rejoined the students. "We've been together for 22 years, and he's been fighting the whole time. I love the sport and I love watching him fight." Her eyes dimmed, her voice lowered. "It's been hard, sometimes, you know… But I've been with him for so long. It's no different for me… My husband's a fighter, I train, and my son will grow up to be a fighter." She smiled and rubbed her belly. Whether she was talking about the son rolling on the mats before her, giggling and screaming, or the one incubating in her stomach, was hard to tell.

Droplets of sweat fell to the mats, shining like bits of glass. The air grew muggy and thick. "Keep it simple," Ludwig repeated, again and again. He often calls things simple. He speaks fast. He jokes and teases. On occasion, he curses. As a teacher, he draws fighters from their comfort zones, switching up their stances, forcing them to advance.

"Forward," he said. "Back… Now right!" There was a corresponding smack of leather. "Simple, no? You know I make that shit look *smooth*."

And yet beneath this lighthearted veneer is deadly seriousness—a respect for the arts that have landed him here. He bows before he leaves the mats to see his family or go to the bathroom; he bows again when he re-enters. After every demonstration, he and Dillashaw bow. You can tell he garners respect from his athletes, and Dillashaw—who unlike Ludwig, is a portrait of intensity at all times—calls him sir.

"He's a technician," says Dillashaw. "He gives us a lot of confidence in our hands and stand-up. He's making it [Team Alpha Male] more of a team—a team atmosphere—instead of a bunch of individuals. We're all working together under Duane."

Starbursts of sweat winked in the lights; wet breath hissed from mouthguards. Bare feet squeaked in sweat on mats—it annunciated the music of glove and grunt like a sharp note, a missed key. Ludwig stepped between them, giving advice, explaining why some things work and others don't. Though he taught the Bang Muay Thai System, he was careful not impose too much of himself on the fighters.

"You gotta find your own style," he says. "We're all individual athletes, and you gotta find what individual style best suits you. So if you can make something work, make it work, that's the best."

He says, regarding striking, "A good striker needs to have the composure to be able to make the strikes that he chooses land. So there's really no right or wrong. You hit and don't get hit and we're good. Of course there are some technical errors, some technical rules, that you should follow, but if you can hit, you can make something work... I think some of the most technically unsound fighters are boxers. Technically, I think a lot of them are horrible, you know, in terms of textbook boxing, but they make it work, and that's what's important."

He describes his own style as technically sound, and you could see this dedication to the basics as he led the seminar, refining position, adjusting footwork.

"Get them tall," he yelled. "Keep them tall. Relax."

After an hour and a half of non-stop training, when the floors were soaked with sweat and the students had to mop it up between sets with toweled feet, they were allotted a brief reprieve. They plopped to the floor and stretched out or walked in circles throwing punches. They talked, they laughed. They watched bright-eyed as Ludwig's children tried on headgear and gloves. At these events, there's none of the posturing you might expect. No showboating, no intimidation. They were comrades, these student warriors; they all shared the desire to learn, to explore their craft—humble, eager, enthused.

"The knowledge they [Ludwig and Dillashaw] bring on the little increments—small little moves, footwork—that can change a fight," said one, writing down what he'd learned in a tiny, sweat-stained notebook. "It's incredible."

The break ended. Now the drills incorporated knees and kicks as well as punches. The students alternated between southpaw and orthodox stances and the sweat dripped with rain-like constancy, covering whole swatches of the mats. Movement and technique were emphasized over speed and power.

"You think you can hit hard?" Ludwig asked, circling a student and peppering him with imaginary punches. "How you gonna fight me? In a real fight, nobody is still."

While his coach expounded on the value of being able to strike and move, Dillashaw broke to throw some combinations at a heavy-bag. Small and lean, Dillashaw is one of several UFC fighters that compose Team Alpha Male, including Urijah Faber, Chad Mendes, and Joseph Benavidez. With the addition of Duane Ludwig, the team has rapidly established itself as one of the pre-eminent forces in the world of mixed martial arts, with all four of the aforementioned athletes coming off impressive victories in their last Octagon outings. Now, with Mendes set to face Clay Guida at UFC 164, Dillashaw fighting in October, Benavidez in September, and Faber having recently bested contender Iuri Alcantara at UFC Fight Night 26, they hope to keep the momentum going.

"We worked a lot on position and footwork," says Ludwig on Faber's performance. "Simple basic stuff—same stuff I teach at my seminars. Making sure we keep our athletic stance and keep him [Alcantara] out of his stance. But it didn't work exactly as planned, and we were able to adjust on the fly... That's what Urijah does; that's what champions do: they adjust on the fly. They make it work. And

that's the thing as a coach: you gotta be able to adjust on the fly too, and not stick with a game-plan if it's not working."

When questioned about a rematch between Chad Mendes and featherweight champion Jose Aldo, Ludwig grins. "One hundred percent" he says. "That rematch is who and what we're gunning for."

But how do you nullify a fighter like Jose Aldo?

"A couple things," he says. "There's a couple openings on him." His smirk widens. "And we'll see what happens when the time comes."

He puts his hands behind his head and says no more.

Dillashaw's fist slammed a dent in the heavy-bag. The class went on. Toward its end, Elite MMA founder and owner Bas Rutten—a one-time UFC heavyweight champion—came in and stood beside Ludwig and watched the trainees. Ludwig, a pupil of Rutten's, stopped what he was doing and took a moment to talk with his old teacher. They compared techniques, each soliciting the opinion of the other, seemingly unaware of the bustling activity by which they were surrounded. They laughed, they exchanged stories. They took in the scene.

It is fitting that the class concluded with these two warriors side by side, surveying the students. Ludwig, in his time, was considered a revolutionary striker, truly showcasing what stand-up could look like in the cage if properly applied. Rutten had had a similar paradigm-setting effect on the heavyweight division. Each helped to evolve the sport to which they'd dedicated their lives. Says Ludwig on the future of striking in MMA:

"The more attention a human being puts into something, the better it gets and the better humans get at it… So it's just gonna evolve like everything, you know… Gets to be that Thai boxing in the UFC is the same level as the European kickboxing at the K-1 level; it's just gonna be like that… Although you can't fight K-1 style in MMA, but everything is going to evolve and evolve in its own way as far as striking in mixed martial arts."

He and Rutten called an end to the class. Gloves tumbled to the floor, shirts peeled off. The trainees stood in a straight and sweating row and faced their teacher. They were silent, drinking water, breathing deeply.

"What was the focus of today?" Ludwig asked.

"Footwork," they answered.

Ludwig smiled. His green eyes shimmered as he looked upon the class. In the abrupt quiet you could hear his children laughing. He bowed, and the students did likewise. Ludwig's gaze lingered on the group a second longer. And then someone was asking for his picture, another for an autograph, another his thoughts on some mysterious technique, and the spell was over.

On the course of his career, Ludwig has no regrets. He says, of his transition into coaching, "I don't really miss fighting. As long as I have that *connection*… I'm living through these guys, now, and it's much easier on me physically and mentally. I love this lifestyle."

He made his way from the class, through the throng of fighters and fans. He moves quickly, his footfalls swift and committed. His eyes look ever onwards, towards the next challenge, the next fight, the next camp. Across his knuckle, his wedding band flickers like a lure and his family walks behind him and behind them Bas Rutten, conversing with T.J. Dillashaw. He has fought and lost and risen above. He has found that peaceful plot for which everyone searches, and so few find.

They call him "Bang."

FIGHTING BEYOND FIGHTING
WHAT MARTIAL ARTS TAUGHT ME ABOUT THE MIND, THE BRAIN, AND OTHER IMPORTANT THINGS

by Jay O'Shea

Maybe it's the warrior spirit. Or plain old aggressive tendencies. But I like to fight. Always have. When I was a kid, fighting wasn't something I did just because I had to. I enjoyed it. The heightened focus, honed attention, and rush of endorphins generated by a physical confrontation produce a euphoria that can't be surpassed. Performance and teaching come close; dancing, onstage or in a crowded class, provides an elevated focus. In all these case, a loss of attention can result in a devastating failure, sometimes with physical consequences. But the stakes go up when someone's fist is headed towards my face.

The unusual thing, I suppose, is that I kept on liking to fight. My love of fighting makes me different from other middle class adults, especially women. Plus, as much as it galls me to admit this, there are people who would consider me middle aged. Apparently, there aren't that many women who continue to love to fight as they move into their fifth decade.

I am also, however, a sensible person with a strong moral barometer. I don't go out of my way to look for trouble and I have a healthy awareness of the dangers of street fighting: court dates, long-term grievances, injury or, in the worst possible scenario, death. I don't embrace ideas like those evoked in Stand Your Ground laws. Escape is always a better option than fighting for ethical and practical reasons alike. Besides, the one time I injured another person in a confrontation – in self-defense, just for the record – I felt a visceral disgust that lasted for weeks. I was as traumatized as if I had been hurt myself.

That's where the martial arts come in. Martial arts training provides the benefits of fighting without the ethical, legal, and emotional consequences of real confrontation. I recognize that violence is wrong at the same time that I see something inherently human or perhaps inherently animal about fighting. What needs to happen for me and, I think, for a lot of other people is to channel aggression into something productive. A live martial arts exchange, be it sparring, grappling, or chi saoing, offers the same heightened focus of a real fight. But if that's all martial arts was about, it would simply be thuggery redirected. And it is so much more than that.

Despite my enthusiasm for fighting, I am no fight champion. I have never even fought competitively. The years that would have been prime for competition were a time I spent dancing and writing, not training in martial arts. My martial arts study has been a side project to dancing, writing, and writing about dance.

Until this year. All this changed when I discovered Jeet Kune Do, the hybrid martial art created by Bruce Lee. JKD rekindled my love of martial arts and turned me from a dilettante into something resembling an avid practitioner. Jeet Kune Do taught me that my love of fighting goes a long way but is no match for real skill. It's shown me that my enthusiasm can be a disadvantage and that my sense of attack was a good place to start but it would ultimately hinder me. I learned that aggression could blind me to strategy, my own or someone else's.

These insights about the complicated relationship between fighting, sparring, and aggression led me to ask what martial arts can teach us about how our minds work. So far, I've come across a few answers to that question, starting with the relationship between martial arts and complex thought. Simulated fighting is so important to mammalian life that the sociologist Gregory Bateson sees it as the primary way in which mammals learn to differentiate between a sign and its meaning. Being able to play fight, as dogs and other mammals do, means knowing the difference between something real (say, an impending bite) and something feigned (teeth placed on another dog's neck in play).

Humans are rare among animals in that we continue to play into adult life. Dogs are another species that play well into adulthood and, interestingly, they do so primarily through mock-combat. I am tempted to make the argument that the more social the species, the greater the need for play and that martial arts are a highly sophisticated means of providing us with combat play.

I suspect that humans also require play well into adulthood because our capacity for abstract thought is greater than other animals'. If Bateson is correct and combat-play undergirds symbolic thinking, then martial arts helps develop abstract reasoning. My experience corroborates this impression: sparring teaches me to read other people and the messages they send. It continually reminds me, in a live setting, of the difference between the real and the contrived. Sparring offers a clear disincentive to getting the messages wrong: if I mistake the fake-out for the real thing or the real thing for the fake-out, I get hit.

Sparring, with its constant use of strategy, fakes, and feints, requires the brain to work at a high level. But I think martial arts have still more to teach us about the workings of our minds (as well as our bodies). Dancers, martial artists, and athletes have long known that we learn movement effectively by watching it as well as by practicing it. Science's discovery of mirror neurons shows us how this works: there are neurons that fire whether an individual is watching a movement or performing it. Likewise, long before I had heard of brain plasticity, I knew, from my dance training, that both the body and the mind were malleable. Well before neuroscience had crossed over into the mainstream, dancers, martial artists, and other physical practitioners knew that learning new movement creates new pathways in the brain. (Neuroscience has provided a more nuanced understanding of muscle memory, suggesting that it is not a pattern but a focused problem solving, not a thing but a capacity.)

By constantly challenging us to create new patterns within our minds and bodies, the practice of martial arts can teach us new ways of moving through the world. Through learning new skills, especially when the stakes are high, we can shift our perception of our environment and our relationship to it. Studying hybrid martial arts is beneficial not just because each martial art prepares us for different fight situations but because they train us for different life situations. Life, like fighting, is fluid. There is no single solution that will work in all contexts. Hence, Bruce Lee's admonition to "be like water."

It's a truism that to learn a martial art is to learn its life lessons. But martial arts don't just provide insight; they offer wisdom through physical practice, where decisions have to be made in real time. The life lessons of the martial arts are present in the movement itself. In martial arts, the concrete and the metaphorical are one and the same. The real and the figurative come together in the martial arts precisely because these lessons are imbedded in the movement and in the mental training that practicing them requires.

For example, my love of fighting is not just literal. In a challenging situation, my first response is to confront. There are benefits to this: it's honest, or at least it seems to be. And I love a good debate. But I tend to take argumentation seriously. I can't just see it as an intellectual exercise. This has resulted in a tendency to step in, confront, and keep confronting.

So, initially, I pursued a martial art that focused on the attack. From my study of Wing Chun Kung Fu, I have learned that, when conflict is inevitable, it's best approached directly. My Wing Chun Sifu, Gary Lam, often said: "If you're going to fight, hit. If you're not going to fight, walk away." The mechanics of Wing Chun support this: put pressure on the centerline, block only to the degree necessary to deflect a strike, and retaliate as swiftly and directly as possible. Wing Chun focuses on hitting rapidly and unrelentingly, blocking only to hit again; it focuses on destabilizing the opponent's balance by challenging his or her physical structure.

Another explanation for the effectiveness of this approach may have something to do with how fear operates in the brain: the parts of the brain that deal with fear are evolutionarily the oldest and most primitive; they are, for reasons of survival, distant from the part of our brain that handles complex thought. Everyone has a startle response; Wing Chun uses that response to subvert the energy of a confrontation. When someone launches an attack, he or she typically expects retreat, shrinking backwards, maybe hands raised in defense. S/he probably doesn't expect the "target" to palm strike his or her nose and chin, doesn't expect a blade hand to the throat, and doesn't expect a series of seemingly never-ending chain punches; s/he certainly doesn't expect all that in succession.

These insights are as useful metaphorically as they are literally. In situations of conflict – verbal as well as physical – sometimes it's necessary to put pressure on the centerline; sometimes it's necessary to deflect only to keep striking. On both the physical and the metaphorical level, these Wing Chun skills work efficiently on an untrained opponent, on one who expects fear and retreat, or on a fighter who relies on large sweeping strikes to generate power. The problem with Wing Chun, as Bruce Lee uncovered, is that being on the attack renders one vulnerable to counter-attack.

Jeet Kune Do radically overhauled my understanding of confrontation. A JKD practitioner sees the opponent's attack as a moment of opportunity. Since JKD is a hybrid martial art, it's worth considering a few of the systems it includes to address the life lessons imbedded within each.

If Wing Chun is about hitting the opponent, boxing – in my admittedly limited experience – is about gauging your opponent, working speed and timing as well as force, and evading until you can get in some highly effective strikes. Boxing is overlooked in our society as a martial art; it is dismissed as a brutal sport. And yet, boxing depends on strategy, it requires a read of an opponent's energy, and it focuses on avoidance as well on attack. In these regards, as well as in many others – the discipline it requires, for instance – boxing is clearly a martial art. The life lesson, for me, from boxing is that conflict – physical or verbal – is not always about being on the attack. It's about being responsive and thinking several steps ahead. Evasion is as important as attack. In life, as in sparring, sometimes rolling with the punches is what will get you through.

From grappling, I have learned that the attack can be used against me. Grappling forms, again in my limited experience, deploy the aikido-like understanding that an opponent's force can be turned back upon itself. In a grappling situation, I frequently find myself trying to overpower my opponent. This use of force works on an untrained fighter. When faced with a skilled grappler, my own forward-energy becomes a weapon against me. Here, too, there is a life lesson: sometimes, metaphorically as well as literally, it is necessary to fight. But attack always contains the possibility that my force will get me thrown to the ground.

I've also learned that, if one solution doesn't work, try another. All martial arts rely on habituation. Martial arts teach technique so that particular strikes, blocks, kicks, and throws pattern themselves into our bodies and so we can use them without thinking. One of the most satisfying sparring moments I've had to date involved using a maneuver I learned from a traditional Kung Fu form: I came at my opponent with a hammer fist, he bobbed and weaved underneath it, I reversed into a back fist, and struck him square in the face. Aside from the sense of thrilled accomplishment I got from this – that sparring partner is pretty good– I also learned that practicing moves via forms and other drills isn't just something we do to build technique and precision. We learn sequences to incorporate movement patterns that we can then use under stress. The more technique we learn, the more options we have in any given situation.

Grappling arts don't tend to use forms but, like other martial arts, they include training in movement sequences that can then be deployed in a live scenario. But grappling makes explicit what other styles assume you'll figure out eventually: if one maneuver doesn't work, try something different. Use the logbook of moves in your brain, scan through it quickly, and try another approach if your first choice of joint lock or takedown doesn't work. Grappling also graphically illustrates what becomes apparent in other styles through live sparring: it's easier to avoid a situation than end up in one and fight your way out.

From Eskrima, the Filipino weapon-based fighting arts, I am learning to trust brain patterning in the face of seemingly ever-increasing complexity. The angles and the spatial patterns of FMA tangle up my thinking. Of course, this is exactly what they are designed to do: scramble the brain of an opponent. That's why it's effective. Gunting – the scissoring motion that is a simultaneous block and attack and that immobilizes a limb or disarms the opponent – seems to be based around this confusion effect. If you can master a movement that it is confusing to your opponent while being seamless and simple for you, how effective is that? No wonder the Filipinos managed to raise hell against their colonizers.

Martial arts are not just about fighting and not just about play. Martial arts are about intentionally creating patterns in the brain, patterns that allow us to fight better but also that allow us to live better. For me, this has meant learning that I don't need to confront all the time. I can roll with the punches, I can use someone else's force against them, or I can simultaneously deflect and move in at once. If need be, I can step in and control the centerline. But I can choose when to go on the attack and when to evade and, once I'm in, I don't have to stay there.

This is the beautiful paradox of the martial arts: practicing fighting can make you a more peaceful person. It can, of course, also backfire: martial art movies and real-life boxer's life stories are rife with images of sport fighters channeling their martial art skills into real fighting instead of channeling their aggression into the art. But when it works, it works well. Partially, this is because practicing martial arts reminds you that anyone can lose a fight. It's a game of strategy and, no matter how good you are, you can always make a wrong decision. But it's also because, at the heart of fighting, is ease: if you can keep your cool with someone's fists flying toward your face, you can keep your cool anywhere.

The study of hybrid martial arts is teaching me to fight as if the outcome didn't matter. I'm learning to stay calm even as I get hit in the head. I continue to treat sparring as a competition at the same time that I am beginning to trick myself into thinking that its competitive aspects don't trouble me. Maybe this is what Bruce Lee meant when he spoke of the art of fighting without fighting. The greatest lesson I have learned from my training is that there is more to martial arts – and to life – than fighting.

This is an excerpt from a forthcoming book by Jay O'Shea entitled
Fighting Beyond Fighting.

Taking on the conventional wisdom that sport fighting is mere glorified brawling, Fighting beyond Fighting suggests that hard-style martial arts have much to teach us about cognition, personal interaction, and what it is to be human. Bringing together personal experience, philosophical debates as to the nature of the self, and scientific theories of brain plasticity, this book suggests that martial arts yield fundamental insights through – not in spite of – their practical fight applications.

RESOLVE

by Devon Robbins

It takes thirty-eight stitches to close the laceration on my cheekbone. The doctor scrubs the Vaseline out of the cut, picks out little pieces of cotton, then starts the first of three layers of sutures. I keep pulling my right hand into a fist, watching the little bone connected to my pinky knuckle click in and out of place as the needle weaves through my skin. Losing hurts, but what hurts most is coming home and having Shannon look at my banged up face and ask, Is it worth it?

It's the way she looks at me when she says it. The density in her eyes brings everything into perspective. In that moment, the dreams I keep chasing feel more like nightmares.

The doctor slides a needle between the knuckles of my pinky and ring fingers to numb me. He sets the broken bone in place and splints me up, tells me I'll have a suspension of ninety days, at least forty-five days with no contact, pending clearance of my right hand by a surgeon.

I'm more concerned about how long I'll be out of work. Stitches aren't cheap, and neither are diapers. Shannon has never asked me to stop, but I know she wanted to after she had the baby. It is a matter of one of us forfeiting our dreams; her dreams of having a normal family, mine of proving everyone wrong.

My first fight happened when I was fifteen. Father and son, no holds barred in the front room of our low income apartment. He smashed a dry bottle of Jim Beam against the wall and told me that I would never amount to anything, that I was a quitter. I told him being a nobody was still better than being a junkie. I knew it wasn't disciplinary after the first punch. He wanted to hurt me. He held me in the corner of the couch where the cushion meets the armrest and packed his knuckles into my eyes until I went unconscious.

I woke up in the hospital with an orbital fracture, barely able to open my one decent eye. The old man disappeared that night. Permanent numbness in the left side of my face is the only thing I have to remember him by.

The doctor gives me a scrip for painkillers, has me fill out paperwork for billing, and I'm on my way. I take a cab back to the venue. The driver shuffles stations, settling on some turn-of-the-century classical piece. Staring out the window, I wonder if the old man would be proud of me. Ten years later, I'm still seeking his approval.

I pay the driver and slip into my beat-down Honda. Home is an hour drive out of the city, an hour of torture on the Honda's frail little engine. My mind refuses to rest, replaying the third round over and over across the sixty-five miles of vacant blacktop. Dead tired, staring into his eyes with my back against the cage, knowing he'd already beaten me. Fighting is the loneliest sport in the world. You learn to keep yourself company so well that you can't escape your own thoughts.

The lights of my little hometown peek out of the valley and I switch my body's cruise control off. Dropping down the hill into town, I slide the shifter into fourth without using the clutch. The move sends a bone-saw rattle up through the shifter into my broken hand and makes my teeth cringe.

They roll up the sidewalks at night in this little town. I pull up to the first red light and muscle memory flips the blinker on. It's been the same route home from the sawmill, every night for going on three years. Shannon is probably waiting for me, drinking coffee in the kitchen with our little boy in her arms, waiting to beg me to give it up.

I click the blinker off and blow through the red light as fast as the old Honda will let me. At the next red light I don't even let off the gas. The excuses are all used up. I tell her records are for DJ's, but she knows better. We both do. The truth is, I can't answer Shannon's questions anymore. I don't know why I keep fighting. It's all I know.

I pull into the empty lot behind the gym and grab my victory joint from the center console. Lighting the joint, I recline my seat all the way back and stare out the open sunroof. The universe stares back at me, its eyes sparkling in the distance like little embers of hope.

Hope.

The word runs circles in my brain, evasive, but staying just close enough to hold on to. It hides behind memories and slowly dissolves. Remembering is a skill that I never learned to use right. Sentimental images of me and the boys flexing on the mats, having beers at a bar after a fight, they fade into a highlight reel of my shortcomings. Blood and drywall dust from knuckles that choose their own coping mechanisms. Holding my eyelids closed while the baby cries, waiting for Shannon to drag her exhausted body out of bed to comfort him.

I lick my fingertips and pinch the cherry of the joint. Maybe the old man was right.

My brain tells me to go home, get some rest, but I'm too afraid. Home is where my fire dies. I take my bag out of the back seat and walk across the lot to the back door. The lights hesitate, flicker, then snap on with a power surge that echoes through open room. I drop my bag at the edge of the mats and kick my shoes off.

This is the sanctuary. I pull my shirt off, carefully avoiding the stitches, then drop my jeans and place them neatly folded on the floor. I pull on my gi; a blood stained Lucky that Shannon gave me for my birthday three years ago, and tie on my faded purple belt. Standing in front of the mirrors that line the back wall, I analyze the reflection, trying to cypher the affliction in the eyes.

Everything slows down and begins to blur together. A single tear escapes my eye and I wipe it away before it has a chance to snuff the tiny ember of hope that's still burning. Then I think of my little boy, and the rent, and all the things that my old man got wrong.

The thoughts fester underneath my skin. I pull the splint off of my right hand and toss it to the floor. My hands ball up into fists and I can see the fighter in the reflection again. An epiphany, like a tidal wave, swallows all the fear and the guilt. It's more than two men locked inside a cage. It's not about pride. It's fighting for something more, for my family and myself. I've been fighting my whole life, both in and out of the cage. If it's not in the cage, it will be at the sawmill, or an office cubicle. The fight doesn't end when you hang up the gloves.

The light in the kitchen goes out as I pull into the driveway. I grab my bag and the envelope with my four hundred dollars and make my way up the drive. On the porch is a rusted coffee can full of half smoked cigarettes. I take one, dust the ash off the filter and light it. The stale tobacco smoke burns deep into my lungs. I take another drag, drop it back into the can, and push the door open.

My inner monologue searches for answers to questions that have yet to be asked as I kick my shoes off and set my gym bag in the coat closet. The sound of the bedroom door closing at the end of the hallway tells me Shannon doesn't feel like talking. I move through the apartment like a ghost, touch a hand to the coffee pot. Still warm. Giving Shannon some time to gather her thoughts, or fall asleep, I pop a couple Advil and head for the shower.

The bathroom light dilates my pupils a little faster than they were ready for. I assess the aftermath; jaundice yellow eyes that match a body covered with bruises in various stages of healing. The doctor's anesthetic shot has run its course, and my heartbeat pulses through my right hand. The old man's nerve damage spares me the pain from the cut on my cheek and I have to actually touch it with my fingers to feel how swollen it is.

When the steam from the shower starts fogging the mirror, I take a deep breath and step into the near-scalding water. Posting my forearms below the shower head, head hanging slack between my shoulders, I let the water run down the back of my neck, rinsing the fatigue down the drain pipe. I wash myself one-handed, then step out onto the cold linoleum floor.

Shannon has my clothes washed and folded on top of the dryer, a blanket folded with a pillow on the arm of the couch. I dress in the dark hallway and walk to our little boy's room. The bassinet lies vacant in the far corner. Everything is in its place— toys in the chest, receiving blankets neatly folded on the shelf above the dresser.

I pull the door closed and stand frozen, hand stuck on the door knob, suddenly feeling like an intruder.

Gently pulling back the blanket, I crawl into bed and place an unsolicited hand on Shannon's stomach. She holds her eyes closed, but I know she feels me. She takes a deep breath and laces her fingers into mine. My jaw clenches as she tightens her grip on my broken hand, but the scent of coconut on her velvet skin smothers the pain.

Warm, moist air glides over our knuckles as she kisses my fingertips. Sparks flow from her lips, shocking me back to life. I'm the husband again. Husband. Father. Fighter. They're really not that different.

"How did it go?" Her voice is small, barely making it to my ears.

My lips don't want to open. I hoped she would start with something easy to respond to, like, I love you, but she's going for the knockout. "It was close. They gave him the decision. Could have went either way." Each sentence is like a noose tightening around my neck.

She lays motionless, quiet, and I can feel her eyes reflecting off the far wall. The rustle of crickets outside the open window breaks apart the static between us. I don't know what else to say, so I hold her loosely in my arms, trying not to speak.

"What are you going to do?" she asks the empty space in front of her.

Work on my takedown defense, is my first answer, work on my guard with the wrestlers in the gym, but I know that's not what she's asking.

"Every long walk is a series of small steps." The quote hanging in my locker isn't as inspiring coming from my mouth.

"Don't get all philosophical on me, Danny." She scoots herself into my chest, squeezing my hand even tighter. "I'm being serious. It's not just the two of us anymore."

Her grip milks a tear from my eye. "I'm not going to just give up on my dreams. I can't just settle. I watched my old man do it when I was a kid."

"You're not your father."

"I'm not a quitter." I say this kissing the top of her head, hugging her against me.

"Is that what this is about?"

"I don't know, maybe it is."

A tiny voice opens up, a tired whine progressing into a cry. Shannon lifts her head and I kiss her behind the ear, tell her, "Let me." I crawl out of the bed and pull the boy out of the bouncer. He doesn't even open his eyes. I lay him on my chest and gently bounce his little body up and down.

"There's a bottle in the fridge." Shannon pulls the blanket up to her chin, watching, trying not to coach me.

Looking over his shoulder, our eyes meet for the first time tonight. I adjust the boy and bend down to kiss her forehead, tell her, "Don't give up on me." And carry the boy to the kitchen.

Six eggs go into the pitcher along with two scoops of protein, milk, peanut butter, and a tablespoon of creatine. I wrap a towel around the blender to muffle the sound. Sipping the shake, I spread peanut butter and jelly across a few pieces of bread, throw two bananas and a couple granola bars into the lunch box. In the coat closet, I grab my running shoes from my gym bag and head outside for some cardio before work.

The smell of wet asphalt saturates the air. I put a whole mile between me and the apartment before even breaking a sweat. On the way back home, I slow to a jog, shadow boxing combinations as the cool autumn air mixes with the sweat and turns to ice.

In the kitchen, Shannon has finished putting together my lunch. I draw a glass of water from the faucet and stare out the window, psyching myself up for another ten hours at the sawmill. After a quick shower, I throw my clothes on and wrap the splint around my broken hand. Shannon comes out of the bedroom, holding the boy in her arms, bottle under her chin. She sees my stitched and swollen face and closes her eyes. She takes in a deep breath, and when her eyes open, her expression has changed.

I grab my lunch box, shove my feet into the steel toed boots, and kiss the little boy's cheek. Shannon tries to smile and runs her fingers through my hair. I kiss her forehead, glide my thumb over her earlobe, and look her in the eyes. I tell her, "Don't give up on me." And I'm out the door.

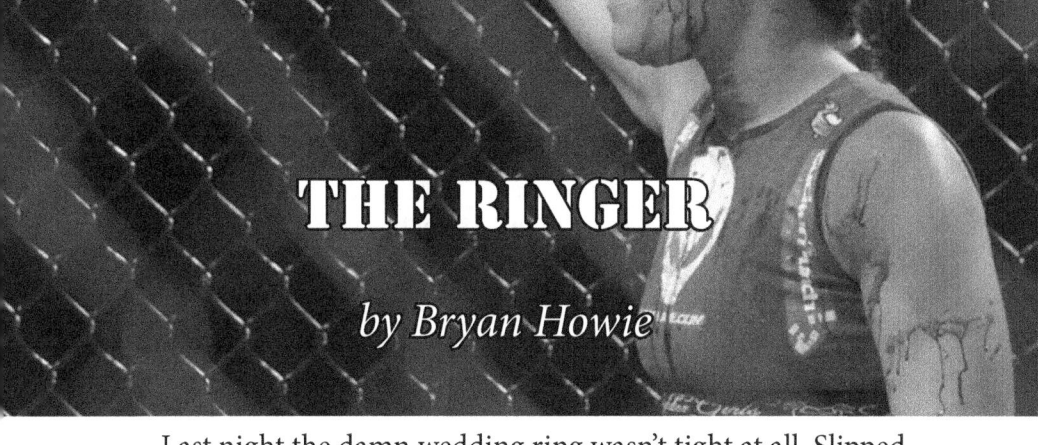

THE RINGER

by Bryan Howie

Last night the damn wedding ring wasn't tight at all. Slipped on and off. I played with it for an hour and rubbed petroleum jelly on my finger to make sure that it wouldn't be stuck today. Sitting in the back of my truck cab on a tiny bed that smelled like cornchips and sweat, I planned. I was ready. I should have left the ring off. But now Mikey looks at my left hand and says, "You're gonna have to take that ring off, Bobby."

"I know." I pull at it, but it won't budge past that fat knuckle. I haven't drank had water all day, but I downed two gallons yesterday. Hydrate first, then let it soak in, but don't go into a fight wet. I don't know if that's good advice, but it's what Blinks told me. And Blinks has been in more fights than anyone I know. Won more and lost more, too.

I'd seen Blinks hit a guy so hard that he pissed his pants. "That's what happens if you go in wet," Blinks said.

The ring is slick, but it won't slide over my knuckle. The skin just lumps up, swollen waves of scar tissue bunching. "Give me a minute here."

"You got about fifteen minutes, easy. But you know we have to get you ready at least two fights early." Mikey waddles across the makeshift locker room like a fat, short clown, but that's bullshit. One hundred percent muscle. I've never seen a stomach bulge with muscle like his does.

The changing room is just a few lockers and a wooden bench. A massage table, a metal wash bin with edges covered with needles, thread, razors, tape, superglue. Tools of the trade.

"Yeah, yeah," I say to Mikey's back as he washes his hands in the sink. Antiseptic, rubbing alcohol, pink towels that used to be white. I stand up and move. Jumping jacks, stretches, punching invisible attackers. Sweat cascades over my finger as I hold it to my neck, counting my pulse, my heart rate stays at a steady 120 bpm. I push against the lockers, stretching my hamstrings, tensing and relaxing my back, holding the poses until an ache forms. Shake it off, twist with my arms swinging. Keep that heart beat up. Sweat and tighten and wring this water out of me. I'm not slacking here, but this fucking ring ain't going to come off without ruining it and that is going to piss off my wife something fierce.

"Get the bolt cutters," Mikey says to his thick-nosed lackey leaning against the door jamb. Guarding it like I was gonna run or something. Then Mikey looks at me with a shrug. "Might not need them, but better to have them here."

The goon smiles. Beneath the dimming, buzzing florescent lights, his white flesh glows sickly green. The goon's teeth glare yellow. Maybe it's the light. Maybe not. The gorilla steps to a hundred-pound punching bag that's covered in duct tape and slicked with lubrication and sweat and anchored to the floor with a heavy bungee cord. He pushes it out of the way like he's pushing a kid on a swing.

I've got to get this ring off before they bring out the snippers.

Can't fight bare-knuckle with a ring on, even if it's just a little gold wedding band. Don't matter a bit. You can wrap your hands with tape, but you have to slick them up with petroleum jelly. It's okay if you make your opponent bleed with force, but if you do it with friction you'll be lucky if you don't get jumped in the parking lot even after the ref has kicked your ass out of the ring.

Mikey walks out. He'll be back after the current fight is over. To get me out there fighting, he'll cut my finger off if he has to. I'd let him if it came to that. I need this fight just like I need every fight. When the door opens, a roar that's always been there suddenly clears into calls for blood, for death, to put that son of a bitch away. Bookies still taking bets. They'll bleed the audience as the audience bleeds the fighters.

Five hundred if I win, two hundred if I lose. I've got every penny from my haul, which is nearly three grand, and every penny set aside for food that's left over bet on me, so that should bring

140

in a total payday of something like ten thousand if I win. If I lose, I'm done. Cut this damn ring off my finger, and I'll be in another hundred just to get the fucking thing re-soldered.

I don't plan on losing, but neither does anyone else. And I'm fighting above my weight. I go in at 195. He's at 225. That's a hell of a difference.

Sitting down on the bench, I wedge my hand between two slats and try to slide the ring off from another angle. It's like trying to shove a couch through a door that's too small. Push this ring from below, slide it from the side, pop the knuckle and push. Nothing going. I'm stuck.

I've got these thick fucking hands. I'm thin, compact, but a bit too tall for my own good. Long torso, short legs. My gut is a target. I've trained myself to take the hits low in my gut. If I see it coming, I'll jump into a fist to make sure it lands right. Fuckers can waste a ton of energy trying to chop me down, but I'm used to it.

But my hands hang like boulders at the end of chains. In some fights, this is an advantage, because I don't have to aim for anything specific. If I'm bleeding into my eyes, I can just jab for the chest and hit the chin half the time. But it also means I can't aim for anything specific. I try to hit the nose, and I'm hitting everything. All the power is spread out. I distribute hurt evenly over a large territory.

The guy I'm fighting tonight, Manny something- Spanish, is the opposite. He's got arms big enough to choke out a python. Shoulders that I can attack all day and never even make a bruise. "He's a big, mean spic," Blinks says. "He's got knuckles like fucking razors. Fucking dangerous cutters."

He's fast and he can aim. I'm taller. I've got the reach and big fists. And if I can sucker him into punching my gut, I can hammer him down. It isn't against the rules to use a hammer-fist to the back of the head, and I can lock my hands together and bring down a shit-ton of force on the crown of a head. I've won fights like that. I've lost fights trying that, too. Leaves you pretty open.

But this fucking ring, if I have to cut it off again, I don't know what's gonna be left of it. Fifty bucks to fix it the last two times, but there's no way it's gonna be that cheap again. It's almost more scar than ring. Clara says go make some money. She says she needs ten thousand dollars to be happy. If I come home with ten grand but with a broken ring, she thinks I've done something to hurt our marriage. She's Catholic, so the bruises and cuts won't bother her but the ring will.

Been gone for six of the seven days this run should have taken, but I got the call last night. Driving a truck all day and night, I get about a thousand miles for every twelve hours. In six days, I'll make three thousand. I drift off into dreams that have me waking up kicking for the brake. I shit and eat when I can, drink beer and sleep when I have to. There's not a lot of money to be made legal.

Never should have married Clara. Never should have married someone I love so much. Blinks says, "Marry someone you can walk away from. Marry a pretty girl you don't like that much. Fuck her a lot. If you want to be in love, find a nice girl to fuck that'll hate you for screwing around on your wife."

I told Blinks that this made no sense. Why wouldn't you just marry the girl you love?

"Never marry someone you love. It puts too much fear in a fighter. You can't fight for love. You gotta fight for yourself. If you can't stand to be a disappointment, you'll never be able to come back from a loss. You're gonna lose. Maybe a lot. And if you fight for that love, every disappointment becomes a failure and then what are you? You start thinking like that, and it's gone."

"You've got it. Right now, you've got it," Blinks said to me. "You know you've got it, but now that you got it, you'll lose a little every day. It never gets better. Love only takes it away all that much faster."

I spit on my hand. I've got a scar from the last time they cut the thing off. It's deep, a gouge. You can't take a wire cutter to a ring that's too tight and expect a gentle cut.

The guy who lived down the street from me when I was a kid used to fight dogs. He didn't have a ring like in the big city. Mostly they were his dogs, a couple dogs brought in by the farmers who thought they had something good. Lockjaws, they called them. Bulldogs that would grab and hold until the body stopped moving. But the dangerous ones, they fought like cats, grabbing and scraping with their hind legs just as much as they fought with their teeth. Mean sons of bitches that would rip a stomach open with a sharpened dew claw or with a lucky lunge to bite the cock off the other dog. Seeing a dog roll in the dirt, bleeding from an open purse where his cocksheath should be, your balls jump up into your stomach and don't come down for a week.

But when his dogs would get tore up, they used old wives' remedies, vitamin K shots, yarrow powder in the wounds, placenta. One guy carried frozen placenta in a zip-lock bag and would feed his female dogs some right before a fight. Said it made them bleed less. Swore by it, but nobody else believed. The coats of those dogs looked great, though.

The guy down the block, his favorite Akita got tore up good on the left flank. Skin and muscle torn open like it had been sliced with a dull knife. Jagged meat. The guy sprinkles cayenne pepper into the wound and the dog relaxes a little. Then he pours honey onto each side of the meat. He closes the wound, rubbing the skin together to make sure it's touching good. Then the son of a bitch takes out some black roofing tar and starts painting the edges. "Works like superglue," he said. "But mom always used this. She knew her shit."

He patted the dog on the rump. The thing just panted and smiled the way a dog will when its master is pleased. The Akita won the fight even with half its ass torn open. Ripped the throat out of a Doberman.

If they cut the ring off, I can use chemicals to make it not bleed, but I just poured superglue in the gouge the last time and it worked fine. It makes for a sore hand and a pissed-off wife, but it don't hurt none. I haven't tried putting cayenne pepper on a wound, though, so I don't know nothing about how well that works. Sounds like it should burn.

These waiting rooms change with every fight. This isn't some fight club, this is underground fighting - very few rules. No weapons, the one rule that matters. That mainly means no steel or reinforced toes. We fight bare-knuckled or with tape wraps, either way you smear petroleum jelly on your fists. Wear shoes so you don't slip in the blood. Elbows, knees, kicks are all legal. Low blows are allowed, but sometimes, if the referee likes you, he'll back the other fighter off long enough for you to take two deep breaths or throw up, but then it's back on. You need more time than that and you're just going to get knocked out.

Once a fighter falls, you can throw a few extra punches. This isn't grappling, but some fights keep going on the ground. If both guys are fighting, they aren't gonna stop it. You try any of those tap-out moves, though, and the boos start and the crowd gets a little wild. You can get a bottle broken over your head for that kind of shit, and nobody is going to care that your scalp is bleeding into your eyes except you.

My hands swell before a fight every time. I should have taken the ring off last night. I know better.

A guy comes in and I can't tell if he won or lost. His eyes are blank with adrenaline, wild and darting around the room, but they aren't seeing anything. They're scanning for movement, for danger. Cats do this when they hunt; mice do this when hunted. His nose is busted and black blood clots crust in his black mustache. Looks like an elbow opened up a cut above his ear, but whether it's just white skin or bone, I can't tell. A shot of epinephrine to staunch all bleeding, probably. His eyes are bloodshot, one front tooth is missing, and his stomach is red with welts and turning purple already.

Then the next guy comes in and I know who the winner is. This guy, he's dead on his feet. Concussed for sure. Both ears dripping blood. Both eyes swollen shut and blood leaking out of his left eye like tears. His body doesn't have a mark on it. The other fighter probably just jabbed a few times, turned the lights out for this guy, and then pummeled him. The guy was probably too stunned to fall down. Happens sometimes. Guys in shock don't know to fall down. The body just stands there, hands lowered, and they take punch after punch.

The refs, they don't stop this. The crowd loves it, and besides, the betting is better on the next round after one of these things.

The matches aren't based on size or strength or skill. I don't know who sets them up. You get a call sometime during the day. Maybe 5 pm, maybe 3 am. A voice tells you the location and the fighter. "Mayfaire warehouse, Manny Whatever. Denver."

"What are the odds?"

"Three to one against you."

I had passed through Denver a thousand miles ago. If I take every penny I have, add in the three thousand I haven't been paid yet, I can triple it. I quit fighting last fight. I'm not the only one who quits fighting with every last fight.

And then you go to the clubs and find out what you're up against. I called Blinks to ask. He knows every fighter within five states. "How the fuck did they match you two up?" he asked.

"One of us is a ringer, I'm guessing." This is an old joke in underground fighting. There ain't no such thing as a ringer in bare knuckles. It's just survival, and nobody I know has any idea how the fighters get matched up.

I think it's a bunch of drunken old fucks setting up these fights, bad gamblers who play the same game we played as kids. Who would win in a fight between Rocky Marciano and Mike Tyson? Between Elvis and Nixon? Between Bush Sr. and Bush Jr?

Rocky, Nixon, Senior.

But now they get to pick two mismatched fighters and send them into the ring. There isn't an actual ring most of the time. Last time it was wrestling mats fenced in with chicken wire. You get knocked against the fence, the crowd pushes you back in. If you don't bleed or draw blood, and it's boos and bottles. You bleed or you're not asked back. Sometimes the loser gets more applause just for being so destroyed.

Two fighters are entering the ring. I can hear the calls echoing into the locker room. The crowd shouts everything from "I love you" to "You're a cunt." You can't please everybody all the time, they say, but here you can't please anyone unless you're dead. You get pulled out of the ring by your feet, and everyone cheers. Then you end up in the river, in an alley, or fed to dogs. The dog fighters get the call first, because nothing makes a dog meaner than eating man. That's what I hear, anyway. I got no money for dog fighting. I ain't got the room, neither.

"It's no fucking good," I say as Mikey and his buddy come back in. The goon's breathing through a deviated septum I can hear even over the crowd. The fight must be a little slow because people are pissed off. "Cut the fucking thing off."

The goon hands Mikey the snippers. He comes at me slow. He does this a hundred times a year. He hasn't ever gouged me before. He aims the cutters to either side of the ring and then puts on enough pressure to keep it in place. Gotta cut length-wise, since he can't get beneath it. I hold my hand steady on my leg.

Clara, she bought this ring. I know some guys buy their own rings when they buy the wife's, but Clara bought this for me before I even proposed. She was a waitress at a strip club at the time, and there wasn't a prettier girl in the room than Clara.

"It's because you can't see my pussy," she told me. "If you could, I'd be just another girl."

I wanted to see her pussy. "When do you dance?"

"I don't," she said, and I'll be damned if she didn't get prettier right then. I can't explain it, because those girls dancing had better bodies and better faces. And I ain't one to judge a person by their job. I was working demolition, tearing down old houses and pulling out the copper and anything else I could salvage. Dirtier work than giving hand-jobs to lonely old men in the dark corners. I could respect a stripper's courage and charity. But that didn't stop me from falling for Clara right then.

"How about-"

"No," Clara said. "You want a coke or a coffee? Free drink with admission."

"Water," I said. And I went back the next night and Clara was waitressing. I only watched her. And tThe next night and she wasn't there, so I left. It took a long time of telling strippers that I was here for Clara before anyone believed I wasn't a liar, a cheapskate, or a pervert.

One night, the bouncers took me out back and gave me a little ass kicking. I took it without throwing a punch. After that, they figured I was okay.

The ring starts to fold under the pressure. The fucking clippers are dull and chipped. "Do it quick," I say.

146

Clara said she bought the ring using only the tips I gave her. That after that second night, she kept every dollar I gave her. She didn't know why, but she thought I was probably a sicko and planned to throw the money back in my face the first time I tried to touch her. But I didn't. So she didn't.

Instead, she ended up buying me a ring.

The clippers click. A slim chunk of flesh goes with it. I grab the ring and open it up. It spreads easily. I almost drop it on the concrete floor. Blood slowly pools in the gash.

A thin line of blood crests the edges of flesh. There's a fight starting. Nobody wants to go seven minutes. Three minutes of bare knuckle is harder than a half-hour of anything else. Three minutes and you start hoping you'll lose just to get out alive. No fight has ever gone to seven minutes. Two fighters throw everything they have at each other for seven minutes and there's not much left to stitch up. The brain dies after that long, and the flesh shows it.

"Shit, Bobby," Mikey says. "I had to do it quick or the ring was gonna twist up. I've never done that before."

"It's fine," I say. "The rings okay. The finger'll heal. Just get me some superglue."

He already has the superglue out and hands it to me. I hold the cap in my teeth as I pour some on my finger. I push the cut closed, hold it in place.

"The crowd's wound tight tonight," Mikey says. "This Manny kid you're fighting..."

He stops. He knows he can't tell me nothing. It might fuck up the bets. I hear the concern in his voice anyway. He's never given a shit for me before, so this is a bad sign.

"Yeah, I'll watch him. Take him out quick. Hope you got money on me."

The goon snorts. Every boxer sounds like a wheezing old dog when they breathe after a while. Broken noses, collapsed septums, shit like that. This guy though, he makes me sick when he breathes. It's like something dried in his throat and there's something wet crawling around in it. It sounds like boot sucking out of mud with a dry cough.

"Probably ten," Mikey says. That's all he'll say. He's already said too much.

The crowd goes nuts. It's fucking anarchy out there and everyone sounds pissed. I cup my hands and hold the broken ring like a holy relic. I line up the cut, push it together. The door opens and in walks a prison fighter. You can spot them a mile away. Useless muscle from working out too much while being locked up and bored. Tattoos that look sore. Even the ink that's beautiful looks red and infected. Always black ink. Heavy-metal ink. The shit might have some seriously fucked up shit in it, scraps of metal maybe because those tattoos never stop being textured and rough.

His black skin is covered in designs. Everything from spiders to angels. He has Christ on the cross on one calf. On the other is a skeleton on a Harley. Never known a black Harley rider. He has the six or seven names on his skin, all of them so fancy that I can't read a single letter. One starts with an F or an S or a T. Across his chest is the only colored tattoo. It looks like he's wearing a necklace made of human ears.

In Vietnam, they say that the guys who went crazy used to collect ears on a string. Have them hang from their belt. The worst would wear it around their necks. The smell of drying, rotting skin and cartilage was supposed to be like a drug. Kept you on your toes. Kept you alive.

This guy, he's too young for Vietnam by at least thirty years. And that's a lot of prison ink - I doubt he's been outside for longer than a month since he was eighteen. His face doesn't have a mark on it. He's not a bleeder. The petroleum jelly is worn off and all that's left is redblack stained tape around his hands.

He can't afford to bleed, I think. The parole officer wouldn't like that.

I kiss the ring then put it in the side pocket of my jeans in my duffel bag. I stand up and start shadow-boxing again. I need my heartbeat back up to 180. Gotta jump and jab, switch stance, jab, cross. Move the head, chin tucked in. Fast as I can, but these melon fists are slowing me down. I weave, I dodge. My body bends well. My back is as strong as my guts.

I imagine the punches coming already. I can see those sharp

little fists breaking against my forearms as I cover my face. Leave the body open. Take those hits in the gut. Just don't let him get my face. He'll slice me open in one hit. Wait for him to put all his weight behind one good gut shot and then bring down my fist like a hammer. Hit him hard enough to knock his spine down an inch. Then back to the guard. Don't get fancy. Just let him dance himself out. Keep the heart pumping, the blood flowing. Keep up, but don't win the fight for him.

The prison fighter, he stares off at a wall, staring through it to something else. I doubt he's here at all, even during the fight. Just instinct for him. He has a long scar over one kidney.

I punch low, which is a fake, punch middle, which is a second fake, and punch high, which is my haymaker. If a guy falls for this, it's lights out with these ham-hocks. Just knocks his head halfway off his body.

I'm warm. The indent of the ring is numb on my hand. My hands are always numb lately. Driving interstate all week will do that to you. My arms are loose and nimble. I feel fast.

The crowd gets louder as the door opens. "Bobby," Mikey calls. Through the door, the hallway, gray walls shine, overexposed to my darkened eyes. I rock my head back and forth, to the sides. I hop my shoulders. Bobby is watching me with those same eyes. "You warm? You ready?"

"Yep," I yell. "Yes. Yup. Let's go." I dance toward the light of the event. I punch the air. I keep focused. I only let myself see my fight. At the doorway, lying on his side, is a large body. A man hovers over the face, slapping the cheeks and waving smelling salts under the crushed nose. I can't see this.

All I see is lights. All I hear is blood. All I feel is fists. All I know is the ring.

ThunderdomePress.com